DEATH OF A PRINCESS

Susan Geason was born in Tasmania, grew up in Queensland, and now lives in Sydney. Most of her professional life has centred on politics and writing, including positions as a researcher in Parliament House, Canberra and Cabinet Adviser in the NSW Premier's Department. Since 1988 she has worked as a freelance writer and editor, including a five-year stint from 1992–1997 as literary editor of Sydney's *Sun-Herald*. Her crime fiction for adults has been published around the world in several languages. Her first book for teenagers, *Great Australian Girls* (1999), was very successful, and was followed by a companion volume, *Australian Heroines* (2001). Her most recent book is *All Fall Down*.

She recently completed a PhD in Creative Writing at the University of Queensland.

Susan can be contacted by email: susan@susangeason.com

DEATH OF A PRINCESS

SUSAN GEASON

Little Hare Books
4/21 Mary Street, Surry Hills
NSW 2010 AUSTRALIA

www.littleharebooks.com

First published in 2005

National Library of Australia
Cataloguing-in-Publication entry

Geason, Susan, 1946– .
Death of a princess.

For children

ISBN 1 877003 90 5.

1. Ramses II, king of Egypt – Family – Juvenile fiction.
2. Princesses – Egypt – Juvenile fiction. 3. Murder – Egypt – Juvenile fiction. 4. Concubinage – Egypt – History – Juvenile fiction. I. Title.

A823.3

Cover design by Serious Business
Cover images: Getty Images
Set in 13.5/17.5pt Adobe Garamond by Asset Typesetting Pty Ltd
Printed and bound in China by Cheong Ming

For Lulu and Rosie Geason

CHAPTER ONE

Meryet-Neith was pleased with herself. The frankincense and myrrh she had bought from the merchant from the Land of Punt were fresh and aromatic, and, after a great deal of haggling, she had obtained them at a fair price. She re-entered the harem through the front gates, passing the massive Nubian doormen, and set off through the central courtyard garden towards her workroom.

Meryet-Neith was a beautician at *Mer-Wer*, the royal harem on a lake in the Faiyum, a fertile oasis south of the Nile Delta. Meryet did not envy the royal wives and children of the Pharaoh, even though she was only a servant. True, the harem was comfortable and its inhabitants wanted for nothing, but—unless Ramses summoned them to one of his palaces—the wives and concubines were not allowed to venture outside the walls as Meryet did, or while away time in the markets of the nearby village. Instead, the world came to them. Local fishermen and farmers supplied them with food and drink, and local craftsmen made their furniture. Merchants from all parts of the Egyptian empire brought luxury goods such as incense, sweetmeats and jewellery.

At fourteen, Meryet was already old enough to be married, and since her birth had been betrothed to Sethi. Sethi was a student of her father, a scribe, and the son of his close friend Ahmose the physician. But Meryet's mother Kiya, who came from a wealthy and influential family in the Upper Kingdom, had arranged an apprenticeship for her at *Mer-Wer* when she had turned eleven. The chance to serve the royal family and learn new skills was a good opportunity for a quick and clever girl, and she was in no hurry to marry and leave her job and the drama and colour of the Pharaoh's harem.

Meryet had learned her skills from Ita, the harem's former beautician. An old woman noted for her perfumes, Ita had taught Meryet how to bargain with the traders from distant lands who sold oils, frankincense and myrrh in the markets, and how to judge the quality of oil and the freshness and strength of incense, herbs and spices by their colour, smell and texture. Meryet had also learned how to extract the scent from flowers to make perfumes; how to blend ingredients to produce scented oils, unguents, soaps and breath fresheners; and how to mix the green and black kohl with which Egyptian women outlined their eyes. Ita also taught Meryet how to dress and curl both natural hair and the heavy wigs the harem ladies wore on special occasions. Since Ita's death a year before, Meryet had become the harem's official beautician.

On the way back to her workroom Meryet thought about the *susinum*, or lily perfume, she was going to make over the next few days. *Susinum* was expensive and complicated to produce, and she'd had to get special permission from Imhotep, the Overseer of the harem, before she could proceed. As well as the myrrh she had just bought, the perfume required other expensive ingredients, including two thousand freshly picked lilies, and the assistance of two servants to strip the leaves from the flowers. Meryet was a little nervous about what she'd taken on, but if she was successful, she knew it would enhance her reputation as a perfumer and bring credit and income to *Mer-Wer*.

Meryet's thoughts were interrupted by the voice of a Hittite woman who attended Princess Isis, one of the Pharaoh's daughters.

"Oh, good, you back at last, Meryet," said Gulikhepa in halting Egyptian. "I look for you. Princess Isis wants you to give massage. Is now convenient?"

It was not particularly convenient, as Meryet had been looking forward to getting started on the *susinum*, but a servant did not refuse an order from the daughter of the divine Ramses II. Meryet bowed and agreed to come as soon as she could.

In her workroom, which was in the same building as the kitchen, the laundry and the food storerooms, Meryet quickly stowed her purchases in the supplies chest. Then she removed her dust-stained linen shift, washed herself over the stone sink and slipped into a clean white shift, fastening it with a belt made of shells. She took a bottle of iris-scented oil from a shelf and placed it in her rush basket beside the other tools of her trade, then made her way to the Hittite women's apartment.

The quarters of many of the Pharaoh's secondary queens were quite small, and the royal concubines and their children were crowded in together, but because she was the daughter of Maathenferure, one of the Pharaoh's Great Wives, Princess Isis enjoyed the use of a large luxurious apartment in the royal wives' wing. Isis's mother—the daughter of the powerful king and queen of Hatta—had been sent to Egypt to marry the Pharaoh in order to cement the peace between the two empires after many years of war. When he saw how beautiful and graceful she was, Ramses II was well pleased with his new bride, and made her a Great Queen. For a time she had lived in the royal palace at Pi-Ramesse with his other Great Queens and their children, but she had ended her days at *Mer-Wer*. According to the harem gossip, the Pharaoh had simply grown tired of her. It was two years now since Maathenferure had caught a fever and entered the Afterlife.

Meryet was fascinated by the exotic apartment of the Hittite women. They had brought their own perfumes, oils, fabrics and carpets from the land of Hatta, and for Meryet it was like travelling to a foreign land without having to leave home. But today the room was in shadow, and seemed to lack its usual colour and vitality. When her eyes adjusted to the gloom, Meryet realised what was different. For a start, the Princess was strangely subdued. The normally lively eleven-year-old lay pale and still on her bed, breathing shallowly. Her chief lady-in-waiting, Lady Matanazi, sat beside her applying wet linen cloths to the girl's forehead.

Isis's two other serving ladies—Gulikhepa and her sixteen-year-old daughter Basemath—sat nearby, sewing silently. This also struck Meryet as odd, for they usually chattered loudly and hounded her for harem gossip and news from the outside world whenever she visited. Basemath looked up, unsmiling, as Meryet entered. Meryet was wary of Basemath, who was, she suspected, a little sly. Her sharp eyes immediately noticed a new turquoise and shell amulet around Basemath's neck. To Meryet it looked suspiciously like one that Maya, the beautiful daughter of the concubine Tuty, had recently lost. Meryet was shocked. *Surely a Hittite lady would not steal a trinket from a concubine's daughter,* she thought. But as was her practice, she guarded her tongue. With so many women confined in one place, all vying for the attention of the Pharaoh to advance their own causes, the harem was a place of jealous intrigue and constantly shifting alliances. Meryet knew it would be dangerous to take sides or to be dubbed a tale-bearer.

Ignoring Basemath, Meryet approached the bedside, bowed, and inquired about Princess Isis's health, as was the custom.

"She has a headache, Meryet, that is all," replied

Lady Matanazi. The lady-in-waiting spoke coolly, but the strain in her face betrayed her concern.

Hearing Meryet's voice, Isis opened her eyes and tried to raise her head. Her yellow-brown cat's eyes were heavy and opaque. "My head hurts, Mery," she said. "Could you rub my arms and legs? They feel strange." The effort of speaking made her wince.

Meryet took out her iris oil, warmed it in her hands, and began to massage the Princess's limbs. Because the Princess loved to adorn herself, she often called on Meryet to paint her eyelids or dress her hair, but Meryet wondered sometimes if it was actually her company rather than her beauty skills that Isis sought. There were many girls of the Princess's age in *Mer-Wer*, but they tended to avoid her because she outranked them. Nobody wanted to risk offending the daughter of a Great Queen, thus bringing upon themselves the Pharaoh's displeasure, although in truth the girl seldom saw Ramses. Besides, from what she heard around the harem, Meryet knew that the Egyptian women regarded Isis as a foreigner, even though she had been born in Egypt. When Maathenferure had died, they had showed little sympathy for her daughter.

Once she had realised that Isis was lonely, Meryet made an effort to overcome her own natural reserve and talk to the girl while she curled her hair and painted her face. She told Isis about her encounters with traders from all corners of the kingdom and about her family, describing their life in the family villa in Thebes, where her father was Chief Scribe in the Ramesseum, the Pharaoh's funerary temple.

Meryet gently rubbed the Princess's limbs in silence. After some time, Isis stirred briefly beneath Meryet's hands, and let out a moan of pain.

Concerned, Meryet looked to Lady Matanazi. "Do you think … Should we call a physician, My Lady?" she asked hesitantly.

"There is no need," the Hittite woman replied shortly. "We have our own ways. You may go now, Meryet." With that, the beautician was dismissed.

Meryet was troubled as she returned to her workroom and put away the contents of her basket. The image of Princess Isis, so wan and still, hovered at the edge of her mind as she prepared the oil for the iris perfume she would begin making the next day. First she bruised cardamom pods and placed them in a bowl of rainwater to soak. Then she poured balanos oil into a pot, added sweet flag and myrrh mixed with wine, and boiled the mixture. When it was thoroughly blended, she strained the oil through fine linen and added the cardamom.

Satisfied, she put the potion aside and made her way to the servants' quarters for the evening meal. She knelt down beside the mat where the food was laid out, picked up a hunk of bread and a bowl of soup, and began to eat. Before long she was joined by Panehesy, a Nubian dwarf who had been abducted from his country by a general and given to the Pharaoh as a tribute. Dispatched to the harem when the royal court tired of him, he was now an attendant to Sitra, a secondary queen who was known to be one of the most difficult women in the harem.

"Hello there, young Meryet," the Nubian said, as he lowered himself to the mat beside her. Meryet and the small black man had become friends when he had asked her to massage his crooked little legs, which often pained him.

"Hello, Nehesy," Meryet responded gloomily.

A quizzical look crossed his dark, wrinkled face when he saw Meryet's tense expression. "You look worried, my girl," he said. "What's wrong?" Intelligent and perceptive behind his playful exterior, the

Nubian had become Meryet's closest confidant in the harem.

Meryet looked around to make sure nobody was listening. "It's Princess Isis, Nehesy," she whispered. "She's ill."

The dwarf soaked up his soup with a chunk of bread. "What's wrong with her?" he asked, cheeks bulging.

"A bad headache."

"Everybody gets headaches, even old Panehesy."

"I know, but I think it's serious—and Lady Matanazi seems worried, too."

"Matanazi knows what she's doing," the Nubian said confidently. "She'll look after the child."

Meryet knew that Nehesy was probably right, but still she was not convinced. "She's not a doctor, Nehesy," she argued. "Sethi's father, Ahmose the physician, says a headache can be a sign of a serious illness."

The Nubian gingerly raised himself from the mat. "Then I'd suggest you keep your eye on her."

Meryet, too, rose to make her way to the servants' dormitory for the night, resolved to keep a careful watch on the young princess's condition.

CHAPTER TWO

Despite her worries about Isis, Meryet-Neith slept soundly and was up at dawn. She hurried to her workroom and took out the oil she had been macerating the night before, strained it, and set the spices aside. Then she poured the remaining mixture into several wide, shallow pottery vessels and set them on a bench beside a jar of honey.

Shortly after, a weather-beaten farmer from a flower farm in the Delta turned up at the gates of the harem with a cartload of a thousand lilies, which were carried to Meryet's workroom in huge armloads and dumped in a heap on the tiled floor. While she awaited the arrival of the two helpers she'd been promised, Meryet turned her attention to a batch of soap ordered by Lady Tamit, the director of the harem's weaving room. In a mortar she pounded natron, a white powder from Wadi Natrun that absorbed grease, lupin seeds to make the mixture lather, and clay to bind the ingredients together. Then she placed the mixture in several pottery jars and set them aside.

By this time, two bleary-eyed girls had appeared at the door. Meryet put them to work stripping the leaves from the lilies and laying the blooms in the vessels that held the scented oil. As the day grew warmer, the aroma of lilies filled the room. Enchanting at first, it soon became cloying and oppressive. Finally, when all the lilies were stripped, Meryet dipped her hands in honey and folded the flowers into the oil. As this concoction would have to sit for a day and a night before the next stage of the process, the helpers' job was done. To their delight, Meryet gave them each a small sample of her famous green eyeliner before thanking them and sending them on their way.

As she was cleaning up, Meryet was distracted by the sound of raised voices in the kitchen nearby. Quietly, she made her way to the door to see what was going on. It was Gulikhepa, Princess Isis's second lady-in-waiting, speaking to Huy, the head cook.

"I must see kitchen," the Hittite woman was saying in her broken Egyptian. "My mistress ill, and Lady Matanazi wants me to see if clean."

Meryet had never seen Gulikhepa assert herself in

this way before. It occurred to her that the Hittite ladies must be very worried about Isis to risk incurring the wrath of one of the most terrifying women in the harem. Large and efficient with small hard eyes, Huy was a tyrant. She bullied her kitchen staff, intimidated her suppliers, and punished her enemies with inedible meals. Now, hands on hips and an angry scowl on her red face, the cook continued to block Gulikhepa's way. "Are you suggesting I keep a dirty kitchen?" she roared.

Gulikhepa's hands clenched, but she stood her ground. "I not accuse anything, Huy. But if Princess to get better, we must know what make her sick." When she realised that Huy had no intention of backing down, the lady-in-waiting said softly, "You want me to tell people you not care about Princess Isis, cook?"

Shooting Gulikhepa a belligerent look and muttering something about foreigners, Huy moved aside.

Meryet watched as Gulikhepa began inspecting the kitchen utensils and the food supplies. Fortunately for the cook, the lady-in-waiting did not find rotting food, dirty utensils or vermin. Meryet had not thought she would; whatever her faults, Huy was a professional. As if sensing her presence, Gulikhepa looked up from the bag of dried beans she was sifting through, and saw Meryet in the doorway.

Meryet bowed deeply. "Is the Princess worse, My Lady?" she ventured.

"Stomach bad, Meryet," said Gulikhepa dismissively. "Not for you to worry."

Meryet knew when she was being told to mind her own business. Bowing again, she withdrew, but she was disturbed by the suggestion that the Princess's condition was worsening. *If I hurry, I can probably beat Gulikhepa back to her quarters and get a look at Isis,* she thought.

Meryet darted along the corridor to the Hittite apartment. Rather than approach the main entrance and chance being seen, she crept to a side door that was screened off by a tapestry. Easing behind the wall hanging, she peeped in. The room had been darkened and the heavy scent of incense could not quite disguise the acrid smell of sickness. When Meryet's eyes adjusted to the shadows, she was shocked by what she saw. The first thing that caught her eye in the dim light was Lady Matanazi, enveloped in a lavishly embroidered ceremonial cloak, prostrate before a statue on a plinth.

Meryet squinted, trying to get a better look at the statue. It was the figure of a woman, richly adorned with gold, silver and lapis lazuli. *This must be one of the Hittite goddesses,* thought Meryet, *and Matanazi is her priestess.*

Between the statue and the priestess, Princess Isis lay on a carpet, asleep or perhaps unconscious—certainly not moving. Suddenly Lady Matanazi stood up. Alarmed, Meryet shrank back against the wall. Then the woman raised her arms and began to chant in a hypnotic voice. From the scraps of the Hatta language she had learned from Isis over the past few years, it sounded to Meryet as if Matanazi was pleading with the goddess Lelwani to cure the Princess. Meryet's skin prickled. To a girl brought up in the religion of Egypt, Hittite gods and goddesses were strange and a little threatening. And for Lady Matanazi to risk praying to alien gods in the harem of the Pharaoh, the God-King of Egypt, Isis must be very ill indeed.

That disturbing thought broke the spell. Slipping out the way she had come, Meryet ran to Queen Sitra's apartment to look for the Nubian. When she did not find him there, she started to search the harem. In the courtyard she came across Maya, surrounded by children and birds. Using seeds, honey and water, she lured the little winged creatures to the courtyard each day, and feeding the birds had become a ritual for the children of *Mer-Wer*. As Meryet looked on, a little girl with gleaming black braids held out her arm and grinned as several larks and thrushes swooped down and perched on it. Even the naked, boisterous little boys with their shaven heads and side curls managed to keep still for Maya's birds.

Maya had a way with animals. As well as her birds, she had adopted a three-legged cat that a kind-hearted servant had rescued from a trap, a shaggy old retired hunting dog that did little but sleep, a mongoose, a flamingo and a shy gazelle. When the birds finally flew away, Meryet approached Maya and asked if she had seen Panehesy.

"I think he's sitting outside the walls," said Maya. "His poor little legs get so sore, you know." She looked around and lowered her voice. "And out there he can get away from Queen Sitra for a while."

Meryet thanked the girl and walked away. She liked Maya, who was always friendly and cheerful, and seemed blissfully unaware of the effect her beauty had on people. Fifteen-year-old Maya was tall and slender, with thick lustrous black hair, perfect skin and large slightly uptilted eyes. But it was her serenity that made her so attractive. How she managed to be so calm with a hopelessly silly mother like Tuty was a mystery to everyone.

At the gates of the harem, the giant Nubian royal bodyguards, the *medjay*, directed Meryet to a patch of shade where the dwarf sat propped against a date palm, his crooked legs stretched out into the sunshine.

"What's up, Mery?" he asked.

"Isis is vomiting now, and Lady Matanazi is invoking Hittite gods to help her."

Panehesy blinked and looked troubled. "Tell me everything."

As Meryet recounted what she had seen and heard, the dwarf's intelligent brown eyes searched her face. "And you're afraid that the Hittite gods might not be strong enough?"

Meryet would not have put it that way, but Panehesy had read her mind. She nodded. "I don't trust their medicine, either. Isis is the Pharaoh's daughter, Nehesy. She should see an Egyptian doctor."

"Like your future father-in-law?"

"Yes. He is one of the Pharaoh's most trusted

physicians." Meryet sat down in the shade beside the Nubian. "I can't understand why they haven't asked for help."

"Perhaps they don't trust *Egyptian* medicine," said the dwarf reasonably. "Or Egyptian gods."

"But we can't just sit by and let her die, Nehesy. We have to *do* something."

Her friend pondered. "Lady Tamit," he said finally.

"You want me to speak to Lady Tamit! I couldn't, Nehesy. I'd be too scared."

Lady Tamit supervised the harem's weaving room. As the Pharaoh expected the harem to support itself and not be a drain on the kingdom's coffers, the royal wives, concubines and various hangers-on were pressed into service producing the fine linen that bore the label of *Mer-Wer*. To make a profit, it had to be run efficiently, and that was Lady Tamit's job. The widow of a rich landowner, she was also the sister-in-law of the Pharaoh's Vizier, who, as Ramses's trusted deputy and chief adviser, was the second most powerful man in the kingdom. In *Mer-Wer* Tamit was his eyes and ears, and the ladies of the harem went in fear of her. So far she had not interested herself in Meryet, and for that the girl was grateful.

"And what if the Princess dies and it's discovered that you knew she was ill?" asked the Nubian.

"But nobody knows …"

"Her ladies know, and if she dies they'll be looking for someone else to blame. And Huy heard you talking to Gulikhepa about Princess Isis's health in the kitchen, didn't she?"

"But it's got nothing to do with me!"

"Mery, everybody knows that your father and Ahmose the physician are like brothers and that you spent half your childhood in the doctor's house. They'll say you should have known enough to take the Princess's illness seriously. You don't have any choice."

Meryet leapt to her feet in agitation. "Couldn't you handle it, Nehesy? Couldn't you drop a word in the right ear?"

The dwarf shook his head. "Tamit would trace it back to me in a trice. Then she'd interrogate me till I told her how I found out. Besides, the information will carry more weight coming from you."

Desperately, Meryet racked her brain for an alternative. For three years she had managed to blend into the background of the harem, going about her duties quietly and making no enemies. Now she was about to be caught between the Hittite women and Lady Tamit and her friends at court, and there was no way she could please both camps. But she couldn't let Princess Isis die.

The dwarf had been studying her face. "So are you going to tell Lady Tamit?"

Meryet nodded apprehensively. "Yes."

CHAPTER THREE

As the Nubian had predicted, Meryet found Lady Tamit in her small office off the weaving room, inspecting the quality of a bolt of snow-white linen. While she waited to be received, Meryet gazed around her. The weaving room was full of minor queens, princesses and concubines, chatting as they worked. Some squatted on the floor spinning flax onto wooden spindles; others knelt before the looms, weaving the linen thread into cloth. Two girls had the job of tying off the loose ends of some lengths of fabric to create the elegant fringe that would adorn the bottom of the most expensive gowns. Several women were passing wooden rods to and fro over the fabric to smooth out the wrinkles. To Meryet it looked like tedious, back-breaking work, and she thanked the gods she was a beautician.

Eventually, Lady Tamit called her in. The middle-aged supervisor of the weaving room was tall and stately, and dressed for work in a simple linen shift.

But Meryet's eyes were drawn to her bracelets. They were magnificent, heavy gold inlaid with precious coloured stones. The jewellery let everyone know that Lady Tamit possessed wealth as well as good connections, and was not to be trifled with—even by the royal wives, who tended to judge people by their status and wealth. Meryet hovered by the door until the older woman condescended to notice her, then bowed deeply.

"So, it's the little beautician," said Lady Tamit in a low cultured voice. "What is it you want, child?"

When Meryet did not reply, the woman stared at her impatiently. "Well, I'm waiting."

Meryet said tentatively, "My Lady, Princess Isis is ill. She has a headache and vomits. She sleeps all the time. I'm worried about her."

Tamit frowned. "How long has this been going on?"

"Two days, My Lady."

Lady Tamit dropped the roll of linen onto a table with an angry thump. "Two days!" She strode to the door and called a deputy over. "Katebet, I have something I need to do. Take over here for me. And you, girl, go back to your quarters and stay there until you are needed." She swept out of the room.

"You heard Lady Tamit, go back to the servants' quarters," said Katebet, a thin sallow woman with a sour mouth and a disposition to match.

Humiliated, Meryet crept back to her workroom. There she paced back and forth nervously, convinced that she had done the wrong thing. The Hittite women would surely guess who had told Lady Tamit about Isis's illness. At last she pulled herself together and set to work straining the lily mixture through a sieve and discarding the liquid. Then she smeared the inside of a clean vessel with honey, sprinkled it with salt and poured in a quantity of balanos oil. As the impurities rose to the top, she skimmed them off with a flat spoon. That done, she placed the strained flowers in a broad vessel, poured in the aromatic oil and added a handful of crushed cardamom. After stirring this thoroughly with her hands she set it aside. An hour later she returned to the lilies and skimmed the froth off the top again. Then she repeated the process of mixing in the oil, cardamom and salt with honeyed hands.

She sniffed the brew. It was coming along nicely, but it was not strong enough yet. It would need at least one more batch of fresh lilies before it smelled right. Tomorrow she would take delivery of another thousand flowers and repeat what she had done today. *If I haven't been sent home in disgrace for offending the Hittite women,* she thought glumly. Afraid to leave the workroom in case Lady Tamit summoned her, she began mixing an unguent scented with iris perfume she had made some months earlier. After what seemed like a lifetime, a servant came to take her to Lady Tamit.

"I've sent someone to fetch Ahmose the physician from Pi-Ramesse," the older woman announced when Meryet appeared at her door. Pi-Ramesse, a city built by Ramses II as his new capital, was where Ahmose lived and practised medicine. "He will be here soon. I want you to tell him everything you have seen and heard. Have yourself ready. We cannot afford to waste time."

Meryet was dismissed. She made her way across the courtyard back to her workroom, where she waited anxiously until a servant came to fetch her. They set off at a trot.

Ahmose was waiting for her in the hallway outside the Hittite apartment. He sketched her a small bow and, although he was not a demonstrative man, Meryet thought he seemed pleased to see her. The doctor was a tall, lean, ascetic-looking man of about thirty-five with a hawk nose, shaven head and piercing eyes. Today his face was stern. "It is not wise to get a reputation for interfering, Meryet-Neith," he said.

Meryet was affronted. Ahmose seemed to think he was speaking to the naïve child who had entered the harem three years ago. She bowed respectfully, but refused to back down. "I would rather that than be known as the one who let Princess Isis die, sir," she said. "You devote your life to healing people. I have acted this way because of what I have learned from you."

Ahmose appeared taken aback by her boldness; he was not accustomed to being challenged by a woman. Meryet waited fearfully for his reaction, but he simply pursed his lips then asked her to describe what she had seen.

Meryet breathed a sigh of relief and told her story. "It started with a headache and lethargy, sir, and she complained of a strange feeling in her arms and legs. When I was in her bedroom yesterday, it smelled of rank sweat and vomit. And Lady Gulikhepa inspected the kitchen to see if the Princess had eaten something bad, but she found nothing amiss. Huy, the cook, is very efficient and keeps a clean kitchen. I know because my workroom is nearby."

Ahmose cleared his throat. "I was wrong to chastise you, Meryet-Neith," he conceded. "You've done the right thing."

On impulse, Meryet asked if she could accompany him when he visited Isis.

"No, that would not be appropriate," he said stiffly. Then he relented. "But don't worry, Meryet, I will do what I can for the little girl."

They were interrupted by the arrival of Lady Tamit, who swept briskly into the corridor. "Come with me, doctor," she commanded, and ushered Ahmose into the Princess's apartment. Over her shoulder she frowned at Meryet. It was time to leave. Meryet pretended to walk away, but when the corridor emptied, she crept to the side entrance of Isis's apartment, slipped behind the tapestry and peered into the room.

Isis was on the bed, writhing in pain and clutching her stomach. Even to Meryet's untrained eye, she looked worse. Ahmose waited impassively while Lady Tamit and Lady Matanazi argued in furious whispers. Lady Tamit must have won the battle, because the Hittite lady-in-waiting withdrew to the back of the room, grim-faced, and stationed herself beside Gulikhepa and Basemath. To Meryet, the Hittite women looked like three stone statues in a shrine. Lady Tamit signalled to Ahmose, who approached Isis's bedside.

The girl opened her eyes. Seeing a strange man alongside Lady Tamit, she became agitated. "Who are you?" she asked Ahmose. As she had never been ill before, she did not recognise the doctor.

"I am one of the physicians of your father the Pharaoh, Princess," Ahmose said soothingly. "He has sent me to make you well."

Is that true? wondered Meryet. She thought it more likely that Ramses was miles away and did not even know his daughter was ill. A messenger was probably galloping the news to him now.

"But I don't know you," quavered Isis.

"I am a good friend of Meryet-Neith, the beautician, Princess," Ahmose said gently. "She is your friend, too, I believe?"

"Where is Mery?" the Princess wailed. "I want her here."

Without thinking, Meryet moved into the room. Lady Tamit looked up in irritation, then beckoned her forward. Meryet ran to the bedside and took Isis's hand. Ahmose started in surprise, but recovered his composure and began his examination of the patient. He felt Isis's skin, looked into her eyes and mouth, smelled her breath and took her pulse by touching a vein in her neck. When he prodded her stomach, which looked swollen and hard, the Princess shrieked in pain.

Meryet saw the doctor pause and frown. His expression frightened her. *Please Horus*, she prayed, *do not let anything be terribly wrong with Isis. She's just a child, and she's never hurt a soul. And she's already lost her mother.*

Finally, the examination was over. Ahmose's face was grave. "I'll prepare some medicine to make you feel better, Princess," he told the girl. "I must leave now, but I'll be back soon to check on you." To the Hittite women he said, "Make sure the Princess drinks plenty of water. And keep her warm." Then he turned to Lady Tamit. "Perhaps Meryet-Neith could stay here, if it makes the Princess happy, My Lady."

Bowing to Ahmose's professional judgment, Lady Tamit nodded her agreement as the doctor left the Princess's apartment. But before departing herself, she drew Meryet with her to the doorway. "I want you to keep me informed of Princess Isis's progress," she murmured. Meryet winced as the woman's fingers dug into her wrist like claws. "If there is the slightest change, send me a message immediately."

Meryet's heart raced. Was Lady Tamit asking her to spy on the Princess?

"I know this is a great responsibility," said Lady Tamit, sensing her disquiet, "but everybody tells me you're a sensible girl and that you know how to hold your tongue. I'm relying on that. Do not let me down."

It was a warning. "May I speak to the doctor?" Meryet begged.

"Be quick."

By this time Ahmose had reached the end of the long corridor, and Meryet had to run to catch up with him.

"Is she very sick?" she asked. "Will she …" The very thought of Isis dying stopped her throat and her voice broke.

Ahmose lowered his voice. "There is still a chance, Mery. She's young and she's been healthy and strong until now. Don't lose hope yet. I'll have Sabni mix up some medicine and send it over." Sabni had been the physician's apothecary for as long as Meryet could remember. "But if she doesn't respond favourably by tomorrow night, you must prepare yourself for the worst," the doctor added.

It was sobering news: if Ahmose and Sabni could not cure Isis, no doctor in the kingdom could. Meryet's hand moved to caress her scarab, the beetle amulet she wore around her neck to protect her from bad luck. "But what is wrong with her, sir?"

"That's the problem," the doctor admitted. "I've never seen an illness like this before."

"Is there anything I can do to help her?"

"Try to keep her spirits up. Don't let her suspect how ill she is or that she might not recover. If her spirits fail, it will hasten her end." Then, speaking softly, Ahmose said, "A word of warning, daughter-in-law. Keep your wits about you. There may be trouble if the Princess dies, so your behaviour must be above reproach …"

Meryet's heart began to pound in fright, but Ahmose had more good advice for her. "Make no enemies, but trust no one either."

☥

When Meryet re-entered Isis's bed chamber, the Hittite ladies were clustered around the girl's bed, bathing her face and cooling her with a peacock-feather fan. *They don't want me here*, Meryet thought.

But, like her, they dared not disobey Lady Tamit. With poor grace they moved aside to let her near, and she took Isis's hand. "Would you like me to rub your back, Princess?" she asked.

"Mery, is that you?" Isis said in a low, weak voice. "I'm so glad you've come back. Yes, please. But be gentle. My skin hurts."

Meryet looked to Lady Matanazi for permission. When the lady-in-waiting nodded, she went to the intricately carved box where the Princess's make-up was kept and looked through the various pots and bottles for a suitable oil or unguent. She discarded any that were too highly perfumed, as they would make the Princess nauseous. In her search, she noticed two items she had not seen before. One was a little limestone jar that held eye make-up. Another was an unguent container with a carved monkey on its side. She sniffed the unguent and did not recognise it; it certainly did not come from her workroom. Eventually she found some oil with a delicate lemony fragrance and returned with it to the Princess's bedside. With a heavy heart she began her massage, trying desperately to will some of her own energy into Isis's limp body.

CHAPTER FOUR

After the massage, Isis fell into a fitful exhausted sleep. Meryet and the Hittite women kept watch by her bed. But the dim closeness of the room and the smell of burning medicinal herbs were soporific, and soon Meryet, too, dozed off. She was woken by the unexpected arrival of Lady Tamit, who was accompanied by Zemti, a high priest at the temple of Horus. Embarrassed, Meryet scrambled to her feet and backed away.

The sight of Zemti was chilling. The gods made Meryet feel very small and powerless, and she was a little afraid of the priests who served them. But the appearance of Zemti was doubly frightening, for he was the most powerful shaman in the kingdom. Lady Tamit—and perhaps Ahmose—clearly thought that Isis's illness was deadly serious. Meryet scrutinised the shaman from under lowered lashes. At first glance he was just another old man, thin and shrunken and browned by the sun, but a closer look revealed an air of authority and calm certainty that inspired confidence. If man's efforts alone could not save Isis, Meryet decided, Zemti might be able to persuade the gods to spare her.

The shaman dropped incense into a censer, lit it, and bent over the sleeping girl. He seemed to be listening to Isis breathe. Perhaps he was measuring the girl's *ka*—her life force. Meryet realised that she had been holding her breath and let out a sigh. Suddenly Zemti straightened up and signalled the ladies-in-waiting to move back. For a time he was perfectly silent and still, as if collecting himself for a great effort. Then he began to recite an incantation to the gods Thoth and Horus. His voice, remarkably powerful for such a slight man, made the hair on the back of Meryet's neck stand up. When he had finished chanting, the priest placed an amulet containing a written spell around Isis's neck and stepped back. The ceremony was over.

Lady Tamit, who had been quiet until now, returned to her normal managing self. "You've done enough here, Meryet," she said. "Get yourself something to eat and go to bed."

"But …"

The woman held up a hand heavy with gold

rings. "Ahmose the physician will be back soon. There's nothing more you can do. The Princess is in good hands."

As there was no point in arguing with a direct order from Lady Tamit, Meryet reluctantly took her leave. Huy had left for the day, so she begged a bowl of lentils and some fruit from Hebeny, a likeable lively girl who worked in the kitchen, and ate it in her workroom. But the drama of the day was catching up with her. Too tired and upset to face the curiosity of her fellow workers in the dormitory, she decided to sleep in her workroom. Heavy-eyed, she had a perfunctory wash, took a sleeping mat and wooden headrest from her storage chest, and lay down on the tiled floor. Embraced by the soothing scent of lilies she immediately fell into a deep, exhausted sleep.

☥

At dawn, only half awake, Meryet took delivery of the second shipment of lilies, and watched the two servants strip the flowers. She was supposed to be supervising them, but her mind was not on her work today; she was preoccupied with thoughts of the

Princess and desperate to know how she was faring. *Surely if anything terrible has happened, they would have told me,* she thought. But her commonsense replied that nobody would think to inform a lowly beautician of the death of a princess.

Meryet was up to her elbows in lilies, oil and honey when a servant appeared at the door and announced that Ahmose the physician was in the harem and wished to speak to her. Her heart immediately started to thud. Would he bring good news or bad? She quickly washed her hands and followed the messenger through the corridors to a large round reception room where Ahmose was waiting impatiently. When the messenger withdrew, he began to speak, but Meryet put her finger to her lips and led him into the courtyard.

"What's wrong?" asked the doctor. "Why have you brought me out here?"

"It's not wise to speak in that room, sir. In some places you can hear people talking in the queens' apartments even though you can't see them, so it's possible they can hear you." She did not tell him that many of the servants referred to the room as the Hall of Whispers. She knew it would sound fanciful to his scientific ears.

But Ahmose was looking ominously grave. "I have bad news, Meryet-Neith," he said sombrely. "The Princess died in the early hours of this morning."

Tears sprang to Meryet's eyes. "But why have you waited so long to tell me, sir? That was ages ago …"

"I've been very busy," Ahmose explained. "You must understand that the death of a princess isn't like the death of a farm worker, or even a scribe or a high priest. It's a very serious matter. And the Pharaoh will want to know what happened to his daughter."

"What did happen, sir? You said you'd never seen such an illness. What did you mean?"

The physician paused, weighing his words. "Let me put it this way, Mery. It doesn't make sense. The Princess showed some signs of fever, but some of the symptoms looked like snakebite."

"But there are no snakes in *Mer-Wer*," protested Meryet.

"I know. And that worries me. If the poison didn't get into her system from a snakebite, how did it get there?"

Meryet was shocked. Ahmose seemed to be hinting that Isis's death might be the work of a human being. But who would dare harm the daughter of the Pharaoh? And why?

"What are you going to do, father-in-law?"

"First I have to explain to the Pharaoh why his physician and a high priest could not save Princess Isis," he said grimly.

Meryet's heart went out to him. How would the Pharaoh react? Would he be grief-stricken, or angry and vengeful? And if he wanted to avenge his daughter's death, on whom would he vent his wrath: the Hittite ladies-in-waiting who had failed to protect Isis, or Ahmose and Zemti for failing to cure her?

Ahmose spoke again. "I am going to make inquiries of my own," he said.

Meryet snapped to attention. "What sort of inquiries?"

"It's better you do not know, Mery. And I'm sure I do not need to warn you not to breathe a word of this to anyone."

Meryet lowered her eyes and held her tongue. She would confide in Panehesy, of course, but Ahmose did not need to know that. He might forbid it. And he might find her close friendship with a Nubian dwarf a little strange.

"Go back to work, Meryet-Neith, and keep your

head down," Ahmose advised. Then, to the girl's surprise, he embraced her. Although Meryet had known the doctor all her life, he had never before shown her any affection. Their involvement in the Princess's illness seemed to have brought them closer. This pleased Meryet. After she married Sethi, they would live in Ahmose's house, and her life there would be much easier if he liked her.

Meryet re-entered the Hall of Whispers, her mind in a whirl. Was Ahmose right? Had someone poisoned Isis? But why—and how? The Hittite women seldom left the Princess alone—not unless she was with someone they trusted. *And I'm one of those people,* Meryet realised with a jolt. The ladies-in-waiting often used her visits as an excuse to venture outside the apartment. A cold shiver ran down her spine. *That means I'm a suspect,* she thought in horror. Then she saw that Ahmose had already worked this out. *That's why he's going to try to find out what really happened. He's frightened for me.*

And now she was frightened for herself. The sound of a voice broke into her reverie. Meryet stood very still and strained her ears. She would know that grating voice anywhere. It was Queen Sitra, scolding someone as usual. Sitra believed that her position as one of the Pharaoh's wives gave her the right to tyrannise everyone in *Mer-Wer*.

"Where is it?" Sitra demanded angrily. "Have you stolen it? If I find that you have been stealing from me or my daughter, I shall have you severely punished."

The victim of this tirade burst into tears and protested that she knew nothing about it. Meryet recognised that voice, too. It was Tiaa, one of Queen Sitra's ladies-in-waiting. The daughter of an influential scribe, sullen Tiaa was betrothed to a wealthy businessman and clearly considered herself too good to be working in a harem. But as royal service would increase her father's influence and bring many benefits to her family, she had no choice but to put up with Queen Sitra's bad-tempered demands.

What is Tiaa supposed to have stolen? Meryet wondered, hurrying away in case the lady-in-waiting stormed from the apartment and caught her eavesdropping. She wasn't sure how long Tiaa would survive. In the three years Meryet had been in the harem, Queen Sitra had gone through dozens of servants. A high-born lady from a rich family, Sitra was ambitious and devious. According to Panehesy, she was continually plotting to bring her daughter,

Neferet, to the attention of the Pharaoh. Anywhere other than *Mer-Wer*, cheerful easygoing Neferet would have been the prettiest girl in any room or even most towns, but here she was overshadowed by Maya, a mere concubine's daughter. Not only was Maya taller and fairer than Neferet, she also played the harp more skilfully and possessed a sweet singing voice. Apparently, the Nubian told her, Queen Sitra feared that beautiful Maya would ruin her daughter's chances of a royal match.

There would be no royal match for Princess Isis now, thought Meryet sadly, her mind returning to the terrible news Ahmose had imparted. She hastened back to her workroom, where the lilies were waiting to be sieved and mixed with oil, but now she was too upset to care. She slumped on the floor against the wall and wept for Isis, who had died painfully and had departed this life far too early. And perhaps a little of her pity was for herself, for Isis's death had reminded her how fragile and fleeting life could be, for princesses and beauticians alike.

☥

Meryet's mourning was cut brutally short by a summons to the apartment of Queen Makare, who wanted a manicure for herself and two of her friends. Meryet obeyed the summons reluctantly, knowing she was in for a merciless interrogation—for word of the Princess's death would have spread by now. The harem's rumour mill ground every snippet of information into a hundred rumours, and by now half of Egypt would know that she had been in the Princess's sick room. The race would be on to drag the details out of her, to embellish them and pass them on.

A vain insensitive woman, Queen Makare came from a very old and respected Egyptian family, and her apartment reflected her rank. Though Meryet disliked the Queen, she had to admit the woman had good taste. The walls were adorned with jewel-coloured woven hangings from Syria and Mittani, and a leopard skin the Queen's father had brought back from the Land of Punt lay over the back of a richly carved armchair. Vibrant carpets covered the tiled floor, ebony statues from Nubia stood on small intricately carved tables, and the scent of aromatic oil suffused the room.

Meryet's appreciation of her surroundings was cut short by Princess Dedi, the Queen's bossy daughter, who ordered her to stop daydreaming and get on with her work. Colouring, Meryet sat down on a low stool at the Queen's feet, took out her manicure kit and picked up the Queen's hand. It was the hand of a pampered pet, soft and slender and a stranger to hard work.

Meryet had been right about the Queen's motives for summoning her, for the women immediately began to bombard her with questions. Meryet felt trapped. Ahmose had warned her to hold her tongue, but she could hardly tell these important ladies to mind their own business. When she could stall no longer, she told them that the Princess's illness had begun with a headache and progressed to vomiting; all she had done was give her a massage to help her sleep. Then she fell silent and applied henna to the Queen's nails.

"Well, girl, go on!" ordered the Queen.

"There is not much more to tell, Your Highness," said Meryet, keeping her head down. "I was not there when the Princess … left us."

Princess Dedi was not satisfied. "You're lying to us, Mery," she said sharply. "You must know more. We've heard that your father-in-law attended the Princess, and that you two were seen talking together."

Meryet's face grew hot. Even if Dedi was a princess, she had no right to bully people who could not fight back. But she hid her resentment. A beautician was expected to know her place. If she showed anger towards her betters, she would be dismissed in disgrace and her family would suffer.

Breathing deeply to steady her voice, Meryet said, "I had not seen the doctor for many months, Princess. He simply wanted to make sure that I was well and happy."

That was true as far as it went. The ladies remained suspicious, but as no amount of persuasion or coercion seemed to work with this obstinate girl, they began gossiping among themselves. Meryet painted and buffed their nails, listening carefully. It quickly became clear that Queen Makare's friends and ladies-in-waiting were excited by the drama rather than moved by Isis's death. From their talk, Meryet picked up the rumours that were flying around the harem: that Isis had contracted one of the fevers that plagued Egypt; that she had been bitten by a snake—though how the snake had come to be in *Mer-Wer* was a mystery; and that she had eaten bad food. The Queen's retinue knew even less than she did, Meryet realised, and had no suspicion of foul play. She silently thanked the gods. If they suspected that a murderer was hiding in the harem, perhaps behind the face of someone they trusted, there would be an uproar. The authorities would launch an investigation, and—Meryet gulped—suspicion would quickly fall on her.

By the time she was finally allowed to go, Meryet was exhausted from the strain of keeping her emotions in check, and her legs felt rubbery as she walked back to her workroom. Tired as she was, she mixed the lily concoction again, in case it spoiled. As she was stirring the mixture, she saw something move out of the corner of her eye. Startled, she turned and found herself staring into the yellow unblinking eyes of a large tawny cat. There were many cats in *Mer-Wer*. Some were workers, employed to keep the vermin under control; others were pets. Meryet did not recognise this animal, but it must have an owner somewhere; it was too well fed and poised to be a stray from the village.

Squatting down, she put out her hand. "Have you run away from home, Miu? Or are you lost?"

The cat stood motionless for a moment, calculating, then cocked its head to one side. The gesture was oddly human, and it gave Meryet an eerie feeling. Then the cat moved and the spell was broken. With a bound, it crossed the room and butted its big head into her hand. It wanted to be friends. When she roughed up its coat and tickled its ears, it purred ecstatically.

"I suppose I should try to find out who you belong to, Miu," she said. The cat gazed at her, as if waiting. "But I'm too tired. You can stay here tonight."

She filled a bowl with water and put it on the floor in the corner, then set off for the dining hall. Though it was getting late, she knew Panehesy would still be there, hoping she would turn up. He would have heard the news by now, and would never pass up the opportunity to question one of the few people in the harem who might actually know what had happened to Princess Isis.

CHAPTER FIVE

Panehesy had finished eating, but had kept a serving of fish stew for Meryet. Until now she had not felt hungry, but the smell of food made her stomach rumble.

"Here, girl," called the dwarf, patting the mat beside him. "Sit down before you fall down."

He managed to contain his questions until she had eaten, but the instant she finished, he demanded to know every single detail.

Meryet recounted the efforts her father-in-law and the shaman had made to save Isis and told Panehesy that Ahmose suspected the Princess's illness was the work of a human, not a god.

The Nubian looked grave. "If Ahmose tells that to the Vizier there will be an investigation. I don't like the sound of that ..." The dwarf was not surprised by Meryet's account of her inquisition at the hands of Queen Makare, or at Princess Dedi's attempt to bully her. "That's typical," he commented. "Dedi is a terror.

Osiris help the man who gets stuck with that one. Mind you, with the amount of sweets she eats she'll probably grow too fat to catch a husband."

Meryet was not interested in Dedi's marital prospects. "What really upset me was that they didn't care that Isis was dead," she interrupted. "They pretended to, but secretly they were pleased. What had Isis ever done to them?"

"You have to know their background," said Panehesy. "Makare's family is very wealthy and powerful and has been for a long time. They don't like the idea of the Pharaoh taking foreign wives because it dilutes the Egyptian bloodline. Complete nonsense, of course. If they shook their own family tree, quite a bit of foreign fruit would fall on their heads, believe me.

"But if I remember rightly, Makare's family lost a couple of young men at the Battle of Kadesh, so they have no reason to like the Hittites. They wouldn't have been pleased when the Pharaoh took a Hittite bride. They're probably relieved that he won't be able to make Isis his wife. And with Isis out of the way, there's one less rival for the Pharaoh's attention."

Meryet was appalled. "But surely he would not choose Dedi, Nehesy! Maya is the most beautiful girl in the harem."

"She's only the daughter of a concubine," Panehesy reminded her. "Dedi is the daughter of a real queen. And so is Neferet, Queen Sitra's daughter."

All this talk of rivalry for the Pharaoh's attention gave Meryet a troubling idea. "Do you think someone would poison the Princess so their daughter would have a better chance of marrying the Pharaoh?" she asked, horrified.

"If they thought they could get away with it. Think how powerful Makare or Sitra would become if they were queens in their own right *and* the mothers of queens."

I might live in the harem, but I really don't have the faintest idea what goes on here, Meryet thought.

"But Princess Isis was too young to be married," Panehesy continued thoughtfully. "So I don't think that could be a reason for wanting to do her harm. Still, I think Ahmose the physician is right to be worried. If there is an inquiry, he'll be in the middle of it. And so will you, Mery."

With a sinking heart, Meryet realised that her friend had reached the same conclusion she had.

"You were in and out of the Princess's apartment before she got sick and while she was dying," Panehesy pointed out. "Everybody knows she trusted you. That means you could have easily given her the poison. I'm afraid you're a natural suspect."

"But what reason would I have to …?"

The dwarf shrugged. "Jealousy? The Princess was beautiful and spoiled and she was the Pharaoh's daughter. You're just the daughter of a scribe, a lowly beautician at the beck and call of your betters. You might have thought that unfair. Or perhaps she complained about your work and you got angry."

Meryet started to protest, but Panehesy raised his hands to stop her. "Of course it's rubbish. I know you loved that poor child, but not everybody in the harem knows you as well as I do. And whoever did it will be looking for someone else to deflect attention from themselves."

Meryet dropped her head into her hands.

Panehesy patted her on the back. "Don't fret, girl. We'll do some investigating of our own."

Together they rose and went outside to find a quiet corner, where they sat in companionable silence. While they watched, a full moon rose over the walls of the harem, illuminating the courtyard and turning the leaves of the date palms to silver. But though Panehesy's voice was still, Meryet could almost feel his mind analysing and plotting away beside her. As for herself, she was too tired to think anymore.

☥

To escape the curious, Meryet again spent the night in her workroom, falling asleep, unwashed, in the clothes she had been wearing all day. She had lurid dreams of being pursued through the corridors of the harem by invisible hostile forces, and was grateful when the racket from the kitchen woke her at dawn. It also aroused the cat, who, she discovered, had spent the night curled up against her body. When she moved, it lifted its head and bumped her on the chin. It was very comforting to have a friend who couldn't ask questions or wonder if she was a secret poisoner, she decided. She scratched its long ears, and it began to purr.

"How am I going to give you up, Miu?" she asked, gazing into its golden eyes. "Let's hope your owners don't track you down too soon. I promise I won't tell anyone you're here if you don't."

CHAPTER SIX

Before she had even had a chance to eat the next morning, Meryet was summoned to the Hittite women's apartment. She found them pale and red-eyed, and dressed in deepest mourning. But she had eyes only for Isis, who was laid out on the bed.

"Mery, we're taking the Princess to the House of the Dead this morning before the sun gets too hot," said Lady Matanazi. "And then we will have to pack up the Princess's belongings. I know that many of the cosmetics in the Princess's make-up chest belong to you. While we are gone, you may go through them and remove anything that is yours."

It was only then that the reality of Isis's death struck Meryet. Never again would she come into these rooms to see the young girl. She would never curl her hair again, or paint her eyelids or colour her nails with henna. Isis was really gone. Tears filled Meryet's eyes. "I'm so sorry, My Lady," she said, her voice breaking.

"I know, Mery," said Matanazi. "I know you cared for the Princess. You were a good friend, and she enjoyed your visits and your stories. Thank you."

At that point, several burly attendants entered the room with a wooden box. Watched closely by the Hittite ladies, they set it down and gently placed Isis's body inside. At a signal from Matanazi, they hefted their pitiful burden onto their broad shoulders and marched out. The Hittite ladies followed them in a solemn procession. At the House of the Dead, they would choose a coffin and speak to the priest in charge about the Princess's mummification.

Once she was alone in the room, Meryet let her tears fall unchecked. When she felt a little better, she began to sort through Isis's cosmetics. Matanazi had been right. In the chest were a pot of kohl and a flask of lotus oil she had used on Isis and forgotten to take away. And there was that unfamiliar unguent pot she had seen before, the one with the monkey carved on it. She picked it up and sniffed. It certainly wasn't one of her scents; she could easily recognise any product from Ita's or her own workshop. This one was quite sweet, but with a slightly bitter bottom note. Meryet shrugged. The Princess must have bought it from one of the traders who brought their wares to the harem, or asked one of her servants to buy it in the village. Meryet was not the only perfumer in Egypt, and many of the royal wives purchased exotic scents from traders or had their menfolk bring them back from trips to foreign lands.

As a professional, Meryet had a keen interest in her competitors' products. What would this one feel like? She was aware that the texture of an unguent was probably even more important than its scent. If it wasn't well mixed, it could be too greasy or lumpy; if inferior oil was used in its manufacture, it could turn rancid on the skin. She looked around. There was nobody about, and no one would ever know she had tried it. But as she was about to scoop some of the mixture onto her finger, a golden object catapulted across the room and knocked the pot out of her hand. It was Miu. Meryet lunged for the pot, but it fell to the floor with a crash and broke in two on the tiles.

Aghast, Meryet stared at the broken pot, and then at the cat. Unruffled, the cat stared back. Hoping no one would come in and catch her, Meryet bent to pick up the pieces. But the cat was suddenly there again, butting her away. Meryet straightened up. "What on earth are you doing, Miu?" she asked, perplexed. "Did you think I would cut my hand? Well, you should have thought of that before you made me break it."

The cat miaowed.

Meryet surveyed the damage in dismay. Should she confess to breaking the jar? No; the Hittite women didn't need any more drama at a time like this, and neither did she. It would be better if she just took the jar away and disposed of it. She found one of Isis's old shawls, threw it over the pot so she would not cut her fingers, and picked up the package carefully. The cat watched intently, poised to pounce. When she had finished, Miu relaxed, sat down on her haunches and began to lick her paws, perfectly calm again.

Feeling a little furtive, Meryet placed the package with the other pots in her apron and returned to her workroom. The cat padded along behind, her tail aloft, waving like a plume. There was no doubt about it, she thought; there was something decidedly odd about this cat's behaviour. She could have sworn Miu had not followed her to the Hittite apartment, but suddenly, there she was. And why had she leapt on Meryet like that? Was it the sight of the monkey on the pot? Had the cat once been frightened, or even bitten, by a monkey? She would never know.

"You were just being a cat, weren't you, Miu," she said.

The cat rubbed against her leg. Laughing, Meryet stowed the cosmetics away in her storage chest. She would dispose of the broken pot later; it could wait, but her lily perfume couldn't. She tested the perfume, adjusted the spices, and gave it a good stir. The cat ambled up to the pan and sniffed the contents. Then, with an approving mew, she retired to a corner to curl up for a nap. *At least Miu has good taste,* Meryet thought.

When Meryet was satisfied with the perfume, she turned to the other work awaiting her. Taking up an elaborate wig owned by one of the older royal wives whose hair was thinning, she started curling some sections and plaiting others into intricate braids. She liked working with wigs. The wooden head that held the wig did not fidget or complain that she pulled too hard. Nor did it talk incessantly and demand attention.

When that was done she looked about for something to occupy her, and decided to make some sweet-breath balls out of myrrh, frankincense, rush nut and cinnamon. But when she went to her supplies chest, she discovered that she had run out of cinnamon bark. For a moment she was discouraged, then she brightened. *Why not go to the markets in the village and buy some?* Perhaps the change of scenery would stop her brooding.

She put on her sandals, ducked into the kitchen to tell Hebeny where she was going, then left the harem. At the gates, the Nubian *medjay*, who remembered her as a friend of Panehesy's, waved her on.

Striding along the dusty road, Meryet wrapped her shawl around her head to keep the sand from blowing into her nose and mouth. At noon in the Faiyum the sun was at its zenith and the glare was painful to the eyes, bouncing off the sand and slanting off the large sapphire-blue lake that abutted *Mer-Wer*. In the distance an ancient pyramid reared golden against the sky, and around it generations of Egyptians slept in their tombs. Workmen scrambled over the nearby temple of the god Herishef, renovating it for King Ramses II.

Just past the temple, Meryet saw a figure walking ahead of her. It was Tiaa, Queen Sitra's lady-in-waiting.

What could Tiaa possibly be up to? Meryet wondered. Ladies-in-waiting were not usually to be found outside the harem walls—especially unaccompanied. Her curiosity piqued, Meryet hurried along after Tiaa, trying to keep her in sight without attracting her attention. As they neared the village, the crowd increased and Meryet relaxed a little. But as Tiaa made her way to the markets, she started to fear she would lose the girl in the crush. At one point Tiaa did disappear, but then Meryet spotted her in the doorway to a building. Shielding her face with her shawl, Sitra's lady-in-waiting was talking animatedly to a middle-aged man whose costume, hairstyle and coppery skin marked him as a foreigner. The stranger had taken up a position where he could see past Tiaa and his head swivelled constantly, surveying the marketplace. Meryet found a shady vantage point from which to watch, but she could not get close enough to hear what they were saying without being discovered.

Though Meryet thought Tiaa's friend looked as if he were up to no good, in the end all he did was pass over a package in return for another small bundle. *All this cloak and dagger stuff for nothing,* thought Meryet sourly, shooing off a particularly persistent fly as Tiaa looked around then hurried back towards *Mer-Wer*. After one last scan of the marketplace, the man disappeared inside the building and closed the door.

Meryet turned her attention to her own business. The market buzzed with colour and noise, with traders and customers haggling over olives and dates, dried beans and barley, salt fish, fresh fruit and vegetables, and clothing and jewellery. There was also a booth with a fortune teller. Meryet found a trader in spices, sniffed her way through his stock and bought some cinnamon bark. It seemed a shame to come all the way to the village and not have a treat, so she bought herself a piece of sticky honey cake from an old woman. Munching on the cake, she gazed longingly at the heavy silver jewellery on a Syrian merchant's stall. He told her he had obtained it from a tribe of desert nomads who dressed in black, lived in tents and travelled constantly with their flocks of sheep.

Eventually Meryet tore herself away and returned to *Mer-Wer*. For the first time, she found herself reluctant to enter the harem. The mysterious death of Princess Isis had unnerved her; the high walls that were meant to protect the Pharaoh's women might in fact be harbouring a killer …

Later in the day, Basemath, the youngest of Princess Isis's Hittite ladies-in-waiting, came to the workroom. Meryet, who had been mixing kohl, stood up respectfully. Though she did not like Basemath, she felt sorry for the girl when she saw how haggard she was from grief and exhaustion. "My Lady?"

"Meryet, Lady Matanazi wants you to go to the House of the Dead for her."

Meryet's heart jumped in her chest. She had heard about what happened to bodies at the House of the Dead. "But why, My Lady?" she asked faintly.

Basemath tossed her head angrily at Meryet's impertinence—servants were supposed to obey without question. "Their Mendesian oil is inferior, and must not be used to embalm the daughter of the Pharaoh and a great Hittite princess."

Scented with cinnamon and myrrh, Mendesian oil was one of the most expensive and rare perfumes in Egypt. Meryet had watched old Ita make it, but had not yet attempted it herself. She knew there were still several flasks of Ita's oil in a locked box in the workroom. Since the old woman's death, only one bottle of the precious stock had been used, for the wedding of a princess to one of the Pharaoh's cousins. But why couldn't they send a servant to deliver the perfume to the House of the Dead?

"You wish me to take it out there myself?" Meryet asked.

"Lady Matanazi needs to be sure the oil gets there safely, Meryet-Neith, and that it is delivered into the hands of Kenamun, the Chief Embalmer," said Basemath importantly. "It must be used on our Princess, and on her alone."

The Hittite ladies did not trust just anyone with such an expensive item, Meryet realised. A clumsy servant might break the perfume flask, or lose it; and a canny one might substitute an inferior brand for the royal Mendesian oil and sell the original. Nor did they trust the embalmers, who might be tempted to use their own second-rate product on the Princess and sell the rare perfume to the family of some rich merchant. No doubt Lady Matanazi had paid the Chief Embalmer to make sure that this did not happen.

Much as she had loved Isis, Meryet's soul shrank at the prospect of visiting the House of the Dead. Her emotions had been in turmoil since Isis's death, and she was not sure her stomach was strong enough for the sights and smells.

Basemath read the reluctance in her face, and looked at her coolly. "Lady Matanazi wishes you to go *immediately*, Meryet-Neith."

Meryet bowed. "If you will allow me, My Lady, I will make preparations."

Basemath withdrew. As soon as she was out of sight, Meryet went to the chest containing Ita's most precious perfumes and took out a bottle of Mendesian oil. After wrapping it carefully in linen, she lay it in her rush basket along with a bottle of water, strapped on her sandals and picked up her shawl. Before leaving the harem, she went to the kitchen and informed Hebeny that, if anybody came looking for her, she would be at the House of the Dead.

CHAPTER SEVEN

Meryet set off with some trepidation. It would be a long hot trek to the House of the Dead, which was located some distance from the village and the harem to prevent the smell of decomposing bodies and the hordes of flies from disturbing the living. She was not particularly brave, and the stories she had heard about embalming made it sound extremely unpleasant. Meryet knew mummification was essential—that the body must be preserved so that the spirit, the *ka*, could enter the Afterlife, a place of pleasure and ease ruled by the god Osiris. She knew in a vague way that she would have to face death and all its duties and rituals when her parents died, but that had always seemed a lifetime away.

Meryet's unease increased as she approached the House of the Dead. The closer she drew to the enclosure where the bodies were embalmed and wrapped in linen bandages, the worse grew the stench. A sudden raucous cry and a flapping of wings made her look up. There was an eagle overhead. She shuddered, imagining what the bird was doing here.

The sun beat down like a hammer on an anvil, and the smell almost suffocated her. Meryet's head spun. She retched into the sand, then covered her face with her shawl.

Straightening up, she saw a toothless skinny man, burned black by the sun and wearing only a skimpy loincloth, watching her. He was laughing. In one hand he held a stick, which he waved threateningly when a kite approached. The bird squawked and wheeled away. "Can't take it, girlie?" the bird frightener jeered.

"Mind your own business, Toothless One," she said coldly. The man just sniggered and ran off after a wild dog that was skulking towards the House of the Dead.

The House of the Dead, Meryet discovered, was a large compound surrounded by a high wall to keep out animals and other predators. When she reached the gate, she noticed a chariot nearby, its horses waiting patiently in the shade of the wall. She thought the rig looked familiar, but was too heat-befuddled to be sure. A doorman who'd been lolling in the shade picking his teeth demanded to know her business.

When she told him, he bade her wait then went inside, returning some minutes later with a priest.

"I have something for Kenamun," Meryet repeated.

"You can give it to me, girl," said the priest dismissively.

Meryet blushed but held firm. "I have strict orders from Lady Matanazi to give it to nobody but Kenamun, sir."

The priest smiled unkindly. "In that case, you'll have to follow me." He turned and headed into the compound.

Meryet drew a deep breath, pulled her shawl over her nose and mouth, and followed the priest. Inside was a series of chambers with thatched roofs and a large open area. She tried to keep her eyes down, but they were drawn against her will to the grisly sights around her.

In the first room they passed, some rough-looking tattooed men were cutting open the body of an old man, busily removing his organs and throwing them into big pottery jars at their feet. Her hand flew protectively to her nose as she saw an attendant stick a long hook up the nose of the cadaver and remove some spongy grey matter. Then she stopped in her tracks. For there on a table, looking very small and lonely, lay Isis. An attendant was washing her naked body.

"Hurry up, girl," scolded the impatient priest, who had moved on. "I haven't got all day."

Though her feet felt as if they were stuck in mud, Meryet tore herself away from the sight of the Princess. In the second room, men were rinsing out a cadaver that had been split open. At a wide wooden table in the next room, a worker was covering a woman's body with a white powder that looked suspiciously like the natron Meryet used to make soap.

Passing some men playing cards in the shadow of a building, they finally found the Chief Embalmer, Kenamun, a tall dignified man with a serious air. He stood to one side talking quietly to another man while, nearby, several workers were bandaging bodies with strips of white linen. Kenamun's visitor was Ahmose. Now Meryet knew why she'd recognised the chariot and horses. As the priest approached the Chief Embalmer to introduce her, Meryet's father-in-law looked up.

"Meryet-Neith, what brings you here?" he asked in surprise. "The House of the Dead is no place for a girl."

"I bring Mendesian oil for Princess Isis from Lady Matanazi to the Chief Embalmer," Meryet explained, taking the precious oil from her basket.

"What was the woman thinking?" her father-in-law muttered to Kenamun, scowling.

The Chief Embalmer shrugged. "She's a foreigner. What can you expect?"

Meanwhile, the heat, the stench and the scenes around Meryet had begun to take their toll.

"The girl is looking rather green around the gills, Ahmose," observed Kenamun. "Perhaps you should escort her home."

Ahmose glanced shrewdly at Meryet's pale face. "She'll be fine as soon as we get away from this place," he said. "But you're right. Come, Mery, I'll take you back to *Mer-Wer*."

Giddy with relief, Meryet followed Ahmose to the gates of the compound and back into the world of the living. The doctor handed her up into the chariot and they set off towards the lake.

When she was far enough away to take a breath without nausea, Meryet asked, "Has one of your patients died, sir?"

"So, the girl is curious," smiled Ahmose. "She must be feeling better."

"I can't
gh stony
Meryet's
weren't
the time
ourt and
uabbles,
was right
with her
e way of
eant for
now that
into the
of *Mer-*
riot, the
our after
of sand.
bout him
washing
iasma of
anic and
o report

aughed.
ld friend of mine. He's also

es how the human body is
doctors can only see the
es the inside too."
need to consult an atom—

d Meryet could see he was
ll her. Then he made up his
opinion about the death of
un agrees with me that
ened to her, I'll report my

d her hand flew to her
me after me, she thought.
en Makare and her family
you think they would harm
at?"
erhaps. But why now? The
n for many years and they
nove against her. If we're
murder, we have to ask who
death."

Meryet shook her head in bewilderment think of anyone."

As they rode on in silence along the rou track, Ahmose's words reverberated in mind. When the wives and concubines working in the weaving room, many spent promoting their own interests in the royal c working on the downfall of their rivals. Sc feuds and plots were common. If Ahmose and Isis's foreign blood had nothing to do death, was it possible that she had got in th another plot, that the poison had been m someone else? But Meryet couldn't imagine poison could possibly have found its way apartment of the well-guarded Princess.

Ahmose and Meryet parted at the gates *Wer*. As she climbed down from the cha doctor advised Meryet to lie down for an h her ordeal. Then he drove off in a spray *Thank the gods for Nehesy*, she thought. *Wit I would be on my own in this place.*

After drinking a huge draught of water, off the sweat, the sand and the lingering m death and decay, Meryet donned a clean t hurried to the Hittite women's quarters that she had completed her mission. Rising from her bow when she was dismissed, she caught a glimpse of Basemath in the background, eating something. When she met Meryet's eyes, the girl composed her face into a serious mask, lowered her hand from her mouth and hid it behind her back. But she was not fast enough; Meryet had seen what she was holding. It was one of Queen Makare's favourite sweets. The Queen bought these expensive sweetmeats from a Palestinian trader who visited the harem only once a year, and hoarded them greedily. She would never have given one to a Hittite woman. Meryet had been right about Basemath: she was not to be trusted.

CHAPTER EIGHT

Meryet was roused from a deep sleep later that afternoon by a servant. Maya wanted to see her. Groggily she splashed water on her face, picked up her beauty kit and followed the girl to the concubines' quarters. There she found Maya holding court with her animals, her three-legged cat purring on her lap and her old dog sleeping at her feet, twitching now and then in some doggish dream.

"Mery, I'm sorry to bother you," said Maya, concern in her voice. "I heard those awful Hittite women sent you all the way out to the House of the Dead." She shuddered. "But Mother thinks that the Pharaoh will come to *Mer-Wer* to attend the funeral of Princess Isis, and is insisting that I start a beauty routine so I'll look my best when he arrives." She touched her face. "She says my skin is becoming rough from spending too much time out in the courtyard with the animals. Do you think she's right?"

"If so, I hadn't noticed," said Meryet diplomatically. "But perhaps you would like a face mask?"

"That sounds wonderful, thank you, Mery." Maya broke off suddenly. "Oh, look, I've got a visitor."

The door hanging parted and Kyky, Queen Sitra's pet monkey, bounded in and leapt to the back of Maya's chair. Sitra indulged the monkey and encouraged his bad behaviour. Meryet suspected she enjoyed watching him torment servants and ladies-in-waiting. Having had her hair pulled and her legs pinched on numerous occasions, Meryet jumped backwards.

Maya laughed. "Don't worry, Mery," she said. "I've taught him to behave when he's in here." Apparently not convinced, the three-legged cat hurled itself off Maya's lap and made for the door. "If he gets up to any mischief, I send him home. He comes here to play with Hunter."

Hearing his name, the old dog raised his head. Kyky immediately clambered down and began stroking Hunter's scarred muzzle. Meryet, who had only seen Kyky at his worst, was amazed by the change in him. Maya must be a miracle worker. When Hunter hauled himself to his feet, Kyky climbed onto his back for a ride around the room. Now Meryet could not help laughing.

"I told you," said Maya. "There's no such thing as a bad animal, Mery, just bad owners."

Quickly bored with that game, Kyky swung himself onto Maya's lap, patted her cheek and chattered away to her. "You want to help me, do you?" cooed Maya.

The monkey danced from foot to foot impatiently.

Maya made combing motions with her hand. "Comb, Kyky."

In a flash of grey fur, Kyky leapt to the floor and filched a comb from Meryet's beauty kit, leaving her open-mouthed. Then he swung back onto Maya's lap, stood up and dragged the comb across the girl's dark curls. Maya clapped, and Kyky did a proud little dance, gibbering excitedly. While the monkey was distracted, Maya took the comb, thanked him, and returned it to Meryet.

"I've never seen Kyky like this before, Maya," said Meryet. "He adores you."

"I know," Maya sighed. "What a pity he's not a wealthy landowner from the Delta. It would solve all my problems. Watch this, Mery." Raising her hand as if holding a mirror to her face, she said, "Mirror, Kyky!"

The monkey ran to Maya's grooming chest and undid the latch easily with his nimble fingers. He rummaged around and returned with a mirror of highly polished bronze, its handle carved in the likeness of the cow-goddess, Hathor. But instead of giving it to Maya as he had done with the comb, Kyky stared into the mirror, entranced by his own reflection, and jabbered away happily.

"He's talking to the monkey in the mirror," said Meryet, amazed.

Maya nodded. "But if I let him go on too long, he'll get jealous and throw the other monkey away," she explained. "Give me the mirror, Kyky," she ordered.

Meryet had been so engrossed in Kyky's tricks that she had forgotten why she was there. She hastily mixed up a purifying mask for Maya. When it was ready, Maya put Kyky on the floor, and lay down on her bed. As soon as she was still, Meryet applied the goo to her face, taking care not to come too close to her eyes and mouth.

"How does that feel?" she asked.

"Lovely," said Maya. "I'll probably fall asleep."

"I'll come back later to take it off and give you a massage," Meryet promised.

☥

Meryet had only just reached her workroom when Hebeny put her head in the door, and said, "One of Queen Sitra's ladies was here looking for you."

Meryet sighed. The last thing she needed was a tense hour with one of the most difficult women in the harem. But to disobey Sitra was to court disaster. She tidied herself up, restocked her make-up kit, and hastened to the royal wives' wing.

Tiaa, Queen Sitra's lady-in-waiting, was in the Queen's apartment mending clothes, a bored expression on her face. When she saw Meryet, she put her finger to her lips and pointed to Sitra's bedroom. "Oh, Meryet, the Queen was looking for you. But please don't wake her," she whispered. "She's been in a dreadful mood all day, and I need a break."

Meryet, still curious about what Tiaa had been doing in the marketplace earlier, saw an opportunity and seized it. "Since she's asleep, would you like me to give *you* a massage instead?" she asked sweetly.

Tiaa's face lit up. "Oh, yes. I'd love one. My skin feels like old leather." She threw down her sewing, peeled off her tunic and arranged herself on a sofa.

Meryet scooped some lotus-scented unguent from a jar with an alabaster spoon, warmed it in her hands, and spread it on Tiaa's back. The girl sighed luxuriously.

"How come your skin is so dry, My Lady?" Meryet asked innocently.

"The Queen sent me to the village in the middle of the day," complained Tiaa.

The Queen sent her? How strange, thought Meryet. "There was no servant she could send?" she prompted.

"Oh, she doesn't trust the servants with large sums of money."

Why would Tiaa have needed large sums of money? Meryet wondered. *Sweetmeats don't cost much.*

"Did she want some of that wonderful nomad jewellery?" Meryet pried. "I'd love one of those silver necklaces myself, but I could never afford it."

There was a pause, then Tiaa said, "No, nothing that interesting. Just some boring old incense from Syria."

The hesitation in Tiaa's voice told Meryet she was lying. *So if it wasn't incense, what was in the packet?*

Her hands moving automatically, kneading the tension out of Tiaa's back, Meryet ran her mind over the events of the last two days. She remembered overhearing Sitra accusing Tiaa of losing or stealing something. Perhaps Tiaa had been sent to the village to replace the item that had gone missing. But what was it? A muffled snore jolted her back to the present. She would find out nothing more here today.

As she was putting the unguent back in her kit, a gleam of jewellery on Tiaa's ankle caught her eye. It was a delicate gold filigree anklet. Meryet crept closer. The anklet looked familiar. But where had she seen it? Then it came to her: it belonged to Queen Sitra. How had a junior lady-in-waiting come by such a valuable object? Even Tiaa, who was impulsive and disobedient, would not dare steal from a queen and flaunt it. That could only mean that the Queen had given her lady-in-waiting the anklet. But why? Such an act of kindness would be most out of character for the imperious Queen. Perhaps Panehesy would know the answer.

Meryet tracked the Nubian down to the harem laundry, where he was gossiping with Baba the manager, a morose old man with a bent back and knobbly knuckles from years spent in damp wash-houses. The laundry was, as ever, a hive of activity. Workers in skimpy loincloths washed garments in vats, rinsed them out in tubs of cold water, wrung them, and hung them out to dry in the sun. Several women were employed pressing the intricate pleats on the dresses of the queens with a special metal iron. Oblivious of the effort around them, the two men were swapping remedies for aching bones.

"I'd better get going, Old Fellow," said Panehesy, finally noticing Meryet waiting for him at the washhouse door.

"Don't forget these," said Baba, handing him some freshly laundered shifts made from the harem's own superfine linen. "Queen Sitra will not be pleased if you return without them."

The two men looked at each other and rolled their eyes. Meryet suppressed a grin. "Let me give you a hand, Nehesy," she offered, for the dwarf was having trouble holding the garments off the grimy floor. She knew Sitra would mete out slaps and abuse for the slightest blemish on one of her expensive shifts.

The dwarf handed over his burden gratefully. "What's new, Mery?" he asked.

Meryet said quietly, "Well for one thing, I've been to the House of the Dead."

The Nubian stopped in his tracks, put his hands on his hips and said angrily, "Who sent you?"

"The Hittite ladies. I had to take some Mendesian oil out there for the Princess."

"They had no right!"

"They're probably not thinking clearly, Nehesy," Meryet argued in their defence. "They're grieving." She grimaced. "And they'd already been out there once themselves. I can't blame them for not wishing to go back."

"But why didn't they send one of their servants?"

"They didn't trust anyone else. They think most Egyptians are thieves."

The dwarf considered that and shrugged. "They're not completely wrong, of course."

Catching sight of Meryet's frown, the Nubian quickly changed the subject. "Have you found out anything interesting since I saw you last?"

"My father-in-law is seeking a second opinion about the cause of Isis's death from Kenamun, the Chief Embalmer."

Her friend nodded in approval. "The more I hear about Ahmose, the more impressed I am. You see why he's done it, don't you? His enemies won't be able to call him a liar if he's got the backing of Kenamun. The embalmer must have seen hundreds of dead bodies, so he'd know if something was wrong."

"That's fine for Ahmose, but what about me?" wailed Meryet in despair. "If the Vizier believes his story, there'll be an investigation, and I'll be a suspect."

"So we had better find the real culprit," said the dwarf. "Have you noticed anyone behaving in an unusual manner?"

"When I saw Basemath today, she was eating one of Queen Makare's sweets. I think she must have stolen it. And I've seen other things in the Princess's room that don't seem to belong there."

"You think Basemath might have poisoned her own mistress?" asked Panehesy, shocked.

Meryet shook her head. "I'm not saying that. I just don't think she's trustworthy or honest. I'm more suspicious of Tiaa, Queen Sitra's lady-in-waiting." She related their conversation in as much detail as she could remember, and described Tiaa's anklet.

"You're right," Panehesy agreed. "She wouldn't wear it in public if she'd stolen it. But why would Sitra give it to her, especially if Tiaa was in trouble for losing something ...?" He stopped, deep in thought. By now they were approaching Queen Sitra's rooms, and he lowered his voice conspiratorially.

"You say Tiaa told you she bought incense from this merchant. What did he look like?"

Meryet described him.

"An Assyrian, by the sound of him," said Panehesy. "He's a long way from home. And they don't make incense in Assyria that I know of. Besides, she could buy the best incense in Egypt from one of the merchants who come to the harem. Or from you."

"The merchant looked as if he was afraid of being seen," Meryet recalled. "He was definitely up to no good."

"So if it wasn't incense, what was it?" the Nubian mused. "Perhaps Tiaa knows. Perhaps she looked in the package and saw something she could hold over Sitra's head, and that's how she got the anklet."

Blackmail! The very thought of a lady-in-waiting having the effrontery to blackmail a queen made

Meryet's heart race. "But what was in the package, Nehesy?"

"That's what we have to find out, Mery."

Suddenly Meryet clapped a hand to her mouth. Maya! She'd promised to return. Calling an apology over her shoulder to the bemused Nubian, she dashed off.

When she entered Maya's room she found her whispering with Princess Neferet, Queen Sitra's daughter. This surprised Meryet, for the girls were supposed to be great rivals. Gathering her wits, she bowed to the Princess and apologised to Maya. "I'm terribly sorry, Maya. I was sidetracked."

"Don't worry, Mery. I've been having a lovely visit with Neferet."

"We've been discussing marriage," said Neferet, blushing.

"It's all we ever do," complained Maya. "If we don't marry, we'll have to spend the rest of our lives cooped up here in the harem slaving under Tamit in that awful weaving room, and being bossed around by our mothers."

"But where are we going to find husbands if we can't marry foreigners?" asked Neferet. "There aren't enough eligible men in Egypt to go around."

"And we're not getting any younger," added Maya.

By this time Meryet had washed off Maya's mask. Her pretty face emerged from under the clay, smooth, soft and glowing. "You're very clever, Mery," Maya said, staring at her reflection in the mirror. "You can make up my face for my marriage to the Pharaoh."

This sent the older girls off into gales of laughter.

"You won't get him, I will," protested Neferet. "At least I will if Mother has anything to do with it. She's already organised the wedding party."

"What about you, Mery?" Maya prodded. "You're promised, aren't you? Have you planned your wedding day?"

Embarrassed, Meryet changed the subject. "Are you ready for your massage, Maya?" she asked.

"Yes, but try this lotus oil that Neferet brought me." She handed Meryet an ornate blue flask. "It's an early birthday present. I'll be sixteen next week."

Meryet picked up the pot and sniffed. It smelled slightly different from Ita's lotus oil, but it was a high-quality product. "What a lovely present," she exclaimed.

Satisfied, Maya lay down on the bed obediently. Meryet knelt beside her and began kneading her arms.

But Neferet was not so easily deflected. "Come

on, Mery, tell us about your future husband," she urged.

Meryet blushed and gave in. "He's called Sethi, Princess. He's the son of Ahmose, the royal physician. It's no great romance. I've known him for years."

"What is he like?" asked Maya.

"He's very intelligent. You have to be to become a scribe. His father wanted him to become a doctor, but Sethi always wanted to be a scholar."

"A scholar," snorted Maya. "They're absolutely useless. I'll bet he's never lifted a finger for himself in his life."

"But scribes are very important," corrected Neferet. "Mery's husband will be a powerful official one of these days."

"Then you'll have to behave yourself, Mery," teased Maya.

"Meryet-Neith will make an excellent scribe's wife," said Neferet, noticing Meryet's blush. "She's very accomplished."

Meryet wondered, not for the first time, how the Princess managed to retain her good nature with a mother like Sitra. "You're very kind, Princess," she murmured.

At that Neferet jumped up. "I'd better get home, Maya. Otherwise Mother will send the awful Tiaa out to look for me. My life won't be worth living if she finds me here with you. I'm not supposed to consort with the enemy."

The Princess's words gave Meryet a chill of foreboding. Neferet was making light of her mother's ambitions, but Meryet wondered if she knew just how unscrupulous Queen Sitra could be. She also suspected that very little went on in the harem without the Queen being aware of it.

CHAPTER NINE

Meryet slept badly that night. In her fitful dreams, monkeys pinched her, dogs barked and menaced her, and eagles swooped threateningly out of a yellow sky. An impossibly tall Lady Matanazi, wearing her embroidered ceremonial cloak, pointed imperiously in the direction of the House of the Dead. Meryet trudged endlessly through the desert under brassy skies, menaced by the bird frightener who chased her and jeered at her fear. In the House of the Dead one of the mummified bodies reared up on its table and pleaded to be taken home. At dawn she woke in fright and was grateful for the sunlight that banished the phantoms of the night.

A breakfast of grapes, figs and bread made her feel a little more human, but her spirits sank again when one of Queen Sitra's rude servants put her head in the door and announced that Princess Neferet wanted a facial. Immediately. Meryet trembled in apprehension, as she always did when she had to face

Sitra. Anything might provoke the volatile Queen. A dropped object or a sudden noise could earn a servant a sharp slap. Sometimes their very existence seemed to annoy her.

But at least Panehesy would be in the room, which was a comfort. The Queen changed her servants as often as her clothes, but Panehesy always survived. He could predict every fluctuation in Sitra's mood and anticipate her every need. And like those small birds that disappear before a storm, the Nubian had the gift of making himself scarce when squalls blew up. Sitra, in turn, trusted him more than she did her ladies-in-waiting; he did not sulk, he was not jealous, and he did not gossip with her rivals in the harem.

Meryet was halfway to the Queen's quarters before she realised that Miu was padding along beside her. "Oh, Miu, you can't come with me this time," she admonished. "The Queen doesn't like cats. And that nasty monkey might hurt you."

The cat gave her a slit-eyed yellow stare, miaowed, and ignored her protest. A passing servant, overhearing this one-sided conversation, looked at Meryet as if she were mad.

I suppose talking to cats is a bit crazy, she thought. But at least Miu listened without interrupting and didn't carry tales. She considered picking up the cat and taking her back to the workroom, but quickly abandoned the idea. As there was no door to her quarters, the cat was unlikely to stay put. She could lock Miu in a cupboard, she supposed, but banished the thought instantly. As she was not at all keen on small, dark spaces herself, she could not do that to a helpless animal.

"All right, I give up," she conceded. "But if you care about me at all, please stay outside in the hallway."

When they reached Queen Sitra's apartment, the cat stationed itself by the door, to Meryet's relief. Taking a deep breath, Meryet entered and looked around. Panehesy was not there! She was on her own today. She felt a little better when she saw that Tiaa and Sitra's other spiteful ladies-in-waiting were also out, probably in the weaving room. Neferet was waiting for her with her face bare of make-up in readiness for the treatment. Queen Sitra, meanwhile, reclined regally on a richly embroidered divan, stroking Kyky's grey fur and popping sweets between his sharp teeth. As soon as Kyky saw Meryet, he tried to jump at her, but Sitra held onto his chain firmly and told him indulgently not to be such a naughty boy.

She was nowhere near as polite to the harem's beautician. "Well, girl, what are you waiting for?" she demanded.

Meryet unpacked her make-up kit and laid out her tools. Then she set to work on Neferet's face. After applying a cleanser and wiping it off with fine soft linen, she covered the Princess's eyes with protective linen pads and began laying a mud mask onto her face with a wooden spatula. This would remove any impurities and tighten up the skin. While she was doing this, a tiny movement, just a displacement of air really, distracted her. It was the cat, creeping into the room. Meryet went rigid and stole a look at the Queen. Thank the gods, Sitra had not noticed Miu. But Kyky had. He watched the cat the way a mongoose would eye a snake, poised to pounce.

Meryet was so intent on the cat and monkey that the Queen's little snore took her by surprise, and she paused, her mud-coated spatula suspended in mid-air. When she'd fallen asleep, the Queen must have released her hold on Kyky's chain, for he suddenly hopped to the ground and sidled towards the cat. Every other animal in the harem screamed and bolted at the slightest scent of Kyky, but Miu did not seem to fear him. Nonchalantly, she began licking her fur.

Baffled, the monkey stopped and stared. The cat finally looked up, yawned widely, got to her feet and padded towards the Queen's bedroom.

Tense as a coiled spring, Meryet resumed applying the mask. Fortunately, the Princess had no idea of the drama swirling around her. Out of the corner of her eye, she watched Miu stroll into the Queen's bedroom. Kyky, too, watched quietly, seemingly hypnotised by the golden cat. Instead of erupting into a ball of flying fur, teeth and claws as Meryet had feared, he let Miu sniff her way around the bed chamber. Finally the cat stopped at a low table by the Queen's bed, and began butting her head against a large jewellery box inlaid with silver and carnelian. Puzzled, Kyky jumped onto the bed and tried to prise open the lid of the box.

Meryet could see that the box was locked, and prayed that Kyky would not start banging it on the floor to break it open, but after pulling impatiently at the lid with his fingers, the monkey swung to another table, scrabbled in a bowl and returned with a key. Clever as he was, however, Kyky could not unlock the box, and he began hitting the lid with the key in a rage. Meryet watched in horror, terrified that the noise would wake the Queen. But suddenly

Miu, bored by Kyky's antics, turned tail and strolled back into the sitting room. Deprived of his audience, the monkey lost interest in the box and followed the cat. Just as Meryet let out a sigh of relief, Kyky realised that nobody was paying him the slightest attention and threw a tantrum. Gibbering angrily, he jumped up onto the divan, landing on the Queen's stomach. Rudely awoken, Sitra lost her temper and dashed the monkey to the floor.

Afraid that Miu would be next, Meryet looked wildly around the apartment—the cat had evaporated like the mist off the river at sunrise. Now that the drama was over, Meryet felt drained. She filed and hennaed Neferet's nails automatically, then washed the mud off the Princess's face and massaged scented oil into her skin. So intent was she on working out the meaning of what she had witnessed that she scarcely heard the Queen's shrill complaints about the monkey. But she could not shake off the idea that the cat was trying to tell her something.

☥

Meryet spent the next morning demonstrating face and body creams, perfumed oils and kohl to two of the Pharaoh's wives. She liked visiting Henttawi and Takhuru, who were young and fun-loving, and Takhuru's delightful little boy, Pamu. By the time the three of them had tried on all her samples and the queens had chosen their favourites, Meryet had almost forgotten that she was embroiled in a plot to murder a princess of the realm.

Not long after she had returned to her workroom, a servant appeared at the door and announced that Ahmose the physician was in the harem and wished to speak to her. Meryet's heart hammered as she ran towards the courtyard, praying he was not bringing more bad news.

She found the doctor staring down into the goldfish pond. He turned when she called his name. His face was grave. Meryet's footsteps faltered and her stomach plummeted. Sensing her fear, Ahmose put his arm around her and drew her into the middle of the courtyard, away from prying ears. "Kenamun, the Chief Embalmer, agrees with me, Meryet-Neith," he said quietly. "We think the Princess was poisoned."

Meryet gave a little moan.

"I'm here to see Imhotep the Overseer," Ahmose continued. "Once he hears what I have to say, he will tell the Vizier. Then the Vizier will want to interview Kenamun and me, and his agents will probably want to question you, Mery. You were with the Princess before she died, so you're a valuable witness. They'll want to know every detail, and they'll keep questioning you until they're sure you're telling the truth. These men have interviewed hundreds of wrongdoers, and have a very good ear for lies or evasions. So get your story straight, daughter-in-law, and stick to it."

Ahmose's words froze Meryet to the bone. "It's not a story, it's the truth! And I didn't do anything wrong!"

"I believe you, Meryet-Neith, because I know you. These men do not. To them you're just another witness—or a suspect. And in a murder inquiry, they can't afford to give you the benefit of the doubt. For all they know, you could be in league with some faction in the harem that hates the Hittites." Meryet's mind flew to Queen Makare and her friends, and their disparaging remarks about Isis's people. "Or you might be the agent of some queen or princess who wants a rival out of the way."

When Meryet began to weep silently, the doctor's usually stern expression softened. "You must keep your wits about you," he told her. "Tell them everything you know. They can't work out who killed your little princess without all the facts." He wiped a tear from her cheek with his finger. "You do want them caught, don't you?"

Meryet nodded, not trusting herself to speak.

"I've sent a message to your parents in Thebes telling them what has happened. Your father is very concerned for your welfare, Mery. He's asked me to make sure you come to no harm, and I intend to carry out his wishes. Now go back to work and try not to worry too much—remember, innocence is the best defence."

As she watched the physician stride off to the Overseer's office, Meryet felt abandoned. How would she get through the day? Work, of course. *I must keep busy or I'll break down,* she told herself. *And I can't afford to do that. Ahmose is right: I have to keep my wits about me.*

☥

The enticing aromas emanating from the pottery jars in her workroom reminded her that she had been neglecting her precious lily perfume. Only a few days ago it had been the most important thing in her life, but since Isis's death she had scarcely given it a thought. It would be a shame to let it spoil, though. Meryet estimated she still had a couple of hours' grace before Maya's appointment to have her eyebrows shaped and her body hair removed. Time enough to finish what she had started.

With two thousand lilies steeped in it, the perfume's scent should be strong enough by now, surely. When a sniff of the mixture confirmed this, Meryet poured it from the large earthenware jars into smaller dry containers, and added crocus powder, crushed and sifted cinnamon, myrrh and water. Later she would skim off the scented oil and decant it into decorative glass perfume bottles smeared with gum and crocus water.

Usually Meryet enjoyed making perfume but today she could not concentrate. She would have to focus herself before she faced Maya, she realised. The hand that tweezed the eyebrows of the harem beauty would have to be as steady as a rock. Meryet darkened her room and sat cross-legged on a mat on the floor, closed her eyes and tried to breathe evenly. Just as she was beginning to feel relaxed a warm weight landed on her lap and snapped her eyes open.

It was Miu. The cat rubbed its golden head under Meryet's chin, then settled down on her lap and began to purr. The low regular sound had a soothing effect, and Meryet began to feel calmer.

But all too soon it was time to go. Meryet picked up her kit, checked that she had the right implements and creams, popped a cinnamon-flavoured lozenge in her mouth to take away the sour taste of fear and fatigue, and hurried to the concubines' quarters.

☥

Hair removal could be a lengthy and painful process. With a long-suffering sigh, Maya seated herself and Meryet set to work. With her she had brought the depilatory preparation that Ita had taught her to make from crushed bird bones, oil, sycamore juice and gum. After heating it up on a small brazier, she began to cover Maya's arms and legs with the paste.

Today Maya's mother Tuty was present, seated on a low chair embroidering a border on the bottom of a linen shift. Although Tuty was overweight—her sweet tooth was legendary—it seemed to suit her, and she was still a beautiful woman. Meryet could see what had persuaded the Pharaoh to make her a concubine, and it was clear where Maya's good looks came from. If Tuty had a fault, besides her laziness, it was loquacity. She was talking when Meryet arrived, and hardly stopped to draw breath for the next half-hour.

Finally, to Meryet's immense relief, Tuty threw down her embroidery, announced that she was going to visit her friend, the concubine Hebrezet, and sailed out. As Meryet continued to apply the paste to Maya's skin, she went over and over the events leading up to Isis's death in her mind. Had she missed some vital clue? Or even worse, had she done anything the investigators might find suspicious?

These dark thoughts came to an abrupt end when Kyky erupted into the room in a blur of noise and movement.

Maya laughed and scolded him. Then she noticed that the monkey was carrying something. "What have you got there, Kyky? Look—it's a pot. Come here and show me. I can't move with this stuff all over me."

But the monkey clung to his pot, and leapt to the top of Tuty's armchair.

"He's just being contrary," Maya explained to

Meryet. "Leave him alone and he'll come down. While we're waiting, would you moisturise my face, Mery? It's as dry as the desert."

Keeping one eye on Kyky, Meryet took out a pot of face cream made from frankincense gum, wax, balanos oil and rush nut. She scooped some out with her fingers and warmed it in her hands before smoothing it onto Maya's face. The monkey watched intently, then reached into the pot he had stolen and, mimicking Meryet's actions, scooped up what looked like unguent and rubbed it on his own face.

Maya laughed. "Whoever owns that cream is going to be upset. Bring it down here, Kyky."

But the monkey ignored her. He swung himself onto the top of a high cupboard, put the pot down, and sat up there chattering away.

Meryet finished moisturising Maya's face, then ripped the depilatory cream, which had set hard, from her limbs. Maya shrieked as the hair came away. But when she felt her skin and found it smooth and hairless, she forgot the pain and was full of praise for Meryet's skill.

While Meryet was massaging iris oil into Maya's skin, the gibbering stopped suddenly. Surprised, the girls looked up. Then, to their horror, the monkey gave a little screech and fell from the cupboard like a stone. His small grey body hit the floor with a sickening thud and lay still.

Maya leapt up. "Kyky!" she cried.

At that moment, Panehesy appeared at the door. He was panting as if he had been running. "I'm looking for Kyky," he said. "He grabbed a pot that Queen Sitra was taking out of her jewellery box, and she ordered me to chase him. She's desperate to get it back, I can tell you!"

Meryet pointed wordlessly at the prone figure. "What shall we do, Nehesy?" she asked.

The Nubian immediately took charge. "I'll take the monkey to the stables. The Stable Master knows about animals. He might be able to help."

Dazed, Maya nodded. She took an old cotton dress out of a drawer and gave it to Panehesy. Gently, he wrapped the alarmingly still monkey in it and carried the sad little bundle away.

"What could be wrong with him?" Maya fretted.

"I don't know, Maya," Meryet replied. "I'll go and see if I can find out." She ran to the stables, where she found Panehesy and Sepi, the Stable Master, bent over Kyky. The monkey was lying on a bed of straw on the ground. In the background a horse stamped and snorted restlessly. Meryet joined the circle around the small animal, who was writhing in pain, his eyes closed.

"The monkey is dying, I think," said Panehesy.

Meryet bent over to look. Then she paused. That was strange. She could smell something vaguely familiar. She sniffed again. Where had she come across it before?

"Move back, Mery," warned Panehesy. "He might rear up and bite you."

"I don't think he's got the strength," commented Sepi, who been a groom in the Pharaoh's cavalry. "His belly's all swelled up and hard. That's the way the nags look when they get colic."

A hard swollen belly? That's what Princess Isis had suffered. "Quick!" said Meryet urgently. "Send for Ahmose the physician."

"For a monkey with colic?" said Sepi doubtfully.

Panehesy looked inquiringly at Meryet. The expression on her face must have convinced him, for he said, "I'm on my way," and sped off.

Muttering that he couldn't understand why they were making all this fuss over a monkey, Sepi stomped off to tend his horses. Meryet was left alone with Kyky, trying to make sense of what had just occurred.

By the time Ahmose arrived two hours later, Kyky was dead. With Ahmose was Kenamun, the Chief Embalmer, who had brought along some of the tools of his trade. From what she'd seen in the House of the Dead, Meryet knew that Kenamun was going to cut Kyky open. When Ahmose suggested she leave, she was only too happy to comply.

She had been pacing the workroom for an hour when Ahmose came looking for her.

"Kenamun and I believe the monkey was killed by the same poison that killed Princess Isis," he announced without preamble. "I've spoken to Imhotep, the Overseer, and he has confined everyone to their quarters. First thing tomorrow, the harem will be searched. If the poison is hidden anywhere in *Mer-Wer*, the Overseer's men will find it."

Ahmose left, and Meryet sat in stunned disbelief, absent-mindedly stroking Miu. Who could possibly want to kill both Princess Isis and a little monkey?

Tired, hungry and afraid, she curled up on her sleeping mat. But despite her tiredness, sleep would not come. The events of the past few days kept replaying themselves in her mind. No matter how hard she tried, she could not make the facts add up. She had never seen Kyky anywhere near Princess

Isis's quarters. Then a picture of the monkey's mean little face rose up before Meryet and it struck her like a thunderbolt. She hadn't seen the monkey near Isis's apartment, but she had seen a monkey pot!

Meryet sprang out of bed, spilling Miu onto the floor, ran to the supplies chest and opened the lid. The monkey pot that Miu had knocked out of her hands was still there, wrapped in its linen rag. As she was about to pick it up, Miu butted her legs fiercely. Then it dawned on her. This had all happened before, in Isis's bed chamber, when she had been about to pick up the broken monkey pot. With a jolt of fear, she realised that the cat had saved her life that day. "Don't worry, Miu. I'm not going to touch it," she promised, slightly breathless. The cat and the girl gazed into each other's eyes, then Miu strolled away.

With infinite care Meryet unwrapped the bundle and examined it. Then, making sure none of it touched her skin, she sniffed the contents. Now she knew why the unguent on Kyky's face had seemed familiar: it was the same as the unguent that she had found in Isis's room!

CHAPTER TEN

Meryet threw on a cotton shift, and cautiously ventured out into the corridor. At this time of the night the harem was dark and slightly sinister and most of its denizens were asleep in their beds. Treading softly, she made her way to the male servants' dormitory. Normally she would never have dared enter such a place, but this was an emergency. Creeping into the room, she searched among the snoring, twitching forms for the Nubian, holding her breath in case any of the men woke and discovered her. When she found Panehesy, she put her hand over his mouth and shook him awake. His eyes flew open in shock, but he relaxed when he saw who it was. Together they tiptoed out of the dormitory into the courtyard, which was cool and shadowy in the magic hour before dawn.

"What in the name of the gods could you want at this hour?" Panehesy asked irritably, running his hands over his face.

"I think I'm beginning to work out what

happened," said Meryet. She told him that she had a pot of unguent in her possession that smelled and looked like the one Kyky had stolen.

"Where did you get it?" he asked, astonished.

"I found it among Isis's belongings after she died," Meryet explained. "Nehesy, I think Kyky died because he rubbed the unguent on his face, and that Isis died from using the same lotion. If the unguent that killed Kyky came from Queen Sitra's room, the one that killed Isis probably did too. All we need to do to prove that is compare the two."

Comprehension began to dawn in Panehesy's eyes. "And if they match, we'll know who did it," said Nehesy.

But something was still bothering Meryet. "I just can't work out why Queen Sitra would want Isis dead," she said.

"What are you getting at?"

"What if it was an accident? What if the poison was meant for someone else?"

"Then how did Isis get hold of it?"

Meryet shook her head. Then, unbidden, a picture formed in her mind—Basemath wearing one of Maya's amulets and eating Queen Makare's expensive sweets. "Basemath stole it. She's a thief."

Panehesy asked the obvious question. "So who was the poisoned unguent meant for?"

"Maya. She's Neferet's real competition, not Isis. I think Kyky got hold of the poisoned unguent meant for Maya."

"So you're saying Sitra had two lots of poisoned unguent," said Panehesy.

"Yes. Queen Sitra didn't know that Ahmose and Kenamun suspected Isis had been poisoned, so she decided to go ahead with her plan to kill Maya. The Queen thought Tiaa stole the first one, so she sent her to the village to replace it. I overheard them arguing, remember. That's what they must have been fighting about."

"And Tiaa must have looked in the package, worked out what was going on and blackmailed Sitra," surmised the Nubian.

"Yes, that's how she got Sitra's gold anklet."

"How was the Queen going to poison Maya?" asked Panehesy.

Meryet described the scene she'd witnessed between the two girls in Maya's room. "Neferet brought Maya a present, some lotus oil, as an early birthday present. Maya's actual birthday is a few days from now."

"A perfect opportunity to give Maya a deadly present," Panehesy cut in. Still thinking it through, he said, "If Ahmose and Kenamun hadn't figured out that Isis was poisoned, Sitra would probably have got away with killing Maya. It would have looked as if both Isis and Maya had died from the same illness." He stopped suddenly, stricken.

Meryet finished the thought for him. "And me, too. If Maya had asked me to apply the unguent, I would have died with her." Her voice faltered as she realised how close she'd come to touching the poison. If it hadn't been for Miu ...

"Don't fall apart on me now, Meryet-Neith," said Nehesy briskly. "We need to report all this to the Overseer immediately and retrieve the two pots. He'll need to send them to Ahmose so his apothecary can analyse it and find out if the two unguents are the same. Then we'll have some evidence instead of just theories."

☥

The harem was turned upside down in the investigation into Princess Isis's death. Nobody in *Mer-Wer* escaped interrogation, neither queens nor princesses nor serving maids. Outsiders such as Ahmose and his apothecary and Kenamun were also questioned, along with villagers who had witnessed the meeting between Tiaa and the Assyrian merchant.

When the case was heard in court, Ahmose and Kenamun testified that they thought Isis had been poisoned, and that the same poison had killed Queen Sitra's monkey. Basemath confessed to stealing the monkey pot containing the original poisoned unguent. (Among her belongings the investigators also found jewellery and amulets that had mysteriously gone missing from the women's quarters over a long period.) Queen Sitra's lady-in-waiting, Tiaa, admitted that she had suspected her mistress of having had something to do with Isis's death; that she had been sent to fetch a package from an Assyrian merchant in the village; and that she had blackmailed the Queen about this. Several witnesses testified that they had seen her wearing Queen Sitra's gold anklet. As well as Meryet, a man and a woman from the village were able to describe the merchant who sold Tiaa the poisoned unguent. The Assyrian himself was long gone.

Panehesy recounted how he had seen Kyky take

an unguent pot from the Queen's jewellery box, and that Sitra had ordered him to get it back. Maya and Meryet told the court how Kyky had become ill immediately after smearing the concoction on his face. Sabni, Ahmose's apothecary, was as certain as he could be that the unguent in the broken monkey pot that Meryet had taken from Isis's room was the same as the one that had killed Kyky.

The murder trial was the talk of Egypt, and the courtroom was packed for Queen Sitra's testimony. She started out defiant and haughty, but as the evidence against her mounted she began to grow frightened. After many hours of interrogation, she broke down and confessed everything. Afraid that Maya's beauty would catch the Pharaoh's eye and that Neferet would be overlooked, she had decided to remove the competition. After hearing about a poison that could be disguised in an unguent, she had enlisted the aid of her brother, a businessman who travelled widely. He had found an Assyrian who would sell them the poison.

Before she could use it on Maya, though, the unguent had gone missing. When she heard about Isis's death she feared that the poison had been involved, and had grown alarmed. But when nobody mentioned poison or came to see her, she thought she'd got away with it and decided to try again. She had kept the second batch of poison under lock and key, waiting for an opportunity to use it on Maya. She had been counting on Maya's death being blamed on the mysterious illness that had killed Isis.

☥

Queen Sitra was found guilty. Under Egyptian law she could have been executed for murder, but the Pharaoh showed leniency and reduced the sentence to life in prison. Sitra was incarcerated in the Great Prison of Thebes, far from the comfort of the harem. Though Neferet was innocent, her mother's actions ruined her. Stripped of her royal rank, she was exiled to a cousin's isolated estate in Upper Egypt. The Hittite ladies-in-waiting were to be sent back to Hattusa—where Basemath would have to face the wrath of Isis's fearsome grandparents, the King and Queen of Hatta—immediately after the funeral. Tiaa was whipped and thrown out of *Mer-Wer*. Ahmose and Kenamun were honoured in a ceremony by the Pharaoh. Maya was heartbroken at Neferet's fate, but grateful to Kyky for saving her life. She paid for his mummification and buried him in her family tomb. That way she and her little grey hero could play together for all eternity in the Afterlife.

Meryet found herself much in demand while the investigation and trial were under way. Ladies who had never required her services before were suddenly fighting over her. This popularity did not last long. Frustrated by Meryet's polite refusal to gossip about the affair, most of them eventually dropped her. This would have upset Meryet in the past, but now she took it philosophically. Although she still enjoyed her work, the harem had lost much of its glamour, and she looked forward to leaving it and embarking on the next phase of her life. Isis's death had taught her that, under the trappings of wealth and power, the residents of *Mer-Wer* were just ordinary people, no wiser or more virtuous than the women in the village down the road.

When Imhotep the Overseer offered her a reward for helping solve the mystery of the Princess's murder, she asked if Panehesy could be freed from slavery. Her wish was granted.

CHAPTER ELEVEN

Seventy days had passed since Princess Isis's body had been dispatched to the House of the Dead for preparation for her burial. During that time the Hittite women, with the assistance of Lady Tamit, assembled the grave goods that she would need in the Afterlife.

Jars of food and wine were collected so that Isis would not go hungry. Her bed, chairs, stools, boxes and chests were readied for her comfort, and her gaming board for fun. Her ladies-in-waiting selected her best wigs and sandals, beaded collars, heart scarabs and amulets made of stone and precious metals. A goldsmith made a gilded funerary mask. Skilled craftsmen were commissioned to produce *shabtis*—the magical figurines of gods and kings made from wood, stone, pottery, bronze, or even wax or glass—that would guard her in her tomb. Because Isis was of royal blood, she was allowed four hundred and one *shabtis*—one for each day of the year, and thirty-six to oversee them.

Meryet had mixed feelings about the funeral. Sometimes she was sorry that Isis had died so young; at other times she was glad that the girl would soon be reunited with her mother in the Afterlife. She was too busy to grieve for long, however, for she had to help assemble the funerary goods. Her job was to decant precious oils and perfumes into bottles and flasks and to fill the Princess's favourite pots and jars with the best unguents, kohl and rouge. And after it was confirmed that the Pharaoh would be attending his daughter's funeral, she was run off her feet beautifying the women of *Mer-Wer*.

Finally the day came when Isis was to be buried in the cemetery attached to the Pharaoh's new temple near *Mer-Wer*. The harem hummed with excitement. Meryet had had a busy morning helping with make-up, and was running late. She put on her finest dress and took special care with her cosmetics—it wouldn't do for a beautician to look anything but her best. The dress, a gift from Lady Tamit and her weavers, was exquisite, with two blue stripes and a gossamer-fine fringe at the bottom. She then outlined her eyes in green and black kohl, and rubbed a little red ochre into her lips. As a final touch, she added a necklace of heavy beaten silver, with lapis lazuli and carnelian beads. It was a gift from her father-in-law to thank her for helping him to bring Queen Sitra to justice.

After slipping into her sandals and adjusting her belt, she ran to the front entrance to meet her parents, and Sethi and his parents, all of whom had been invited to the funeral. Her father had attended part of the trial, but she had not seen her mother for a long time. After she had rushed into Kiya's arms and they had embraced, her mother held her at arm's-length. "You look different, Mery," she said, sounding both pleased and sad. "You've grown up while I wasn't looking."

Sethi seemed to think so, too. Several times that day Meryet caught him gazing at her. There was something different in the way he looked at her now, as if he was seeing her for the first time. It made her spine tingle and her face flush. When she found the courage to scrutinise him, she saw that Sethi was finally growing into his height, and no longer looked like a gangling boy. Indeed, he had become quite handsome since she had last seen him. The prospect of leaving the harem and becoming his wife suddenly seemed more appealing.

It was bedlam in the courtyard where the funeral procession was assembling. Standing patiently with their handlers, a team of oxen waited to pull the sled that would carry the boat-shaped bier holding Isis's coffin. Mourners milled about, talking quietly. A group of priests kept solemnly to themselves. Meryet's eyes widened when she spotted the *tekenu*, a mysterious man enveloped in a cloak, and several *muu* dancers wearing kilts and tall white headdresses. When she tore her eyes away she saw Panehesy and waved. She wished the Nubian could walk beside her, but protocol forbade it. He would have to make up the rear of the procession with the other harem servants. Though she was herself a servant, today Meryet would accompany her parents and in-laws.

A hush fell over the gathering as the two giant Nubian *medjay* arrived with Isis's coffin, which had been resting in the Hittite apartments. The coffin, which was decorated with a brightly painted likeness of the Princess and various pictures of gods and magic spells, was placed inside a flower-bedecked shrine on the bier. Before the sled began to move, two women fell in behind it. These were the professional mourners, representing the two birds of prey, Isis and Nephthys, who had screeched over the body of the god Osiris. They would act out the sorrow and pain of the mourners.

The priests went to the front of the bier, and the mourners lined up behind in order of rank, with members of the royal family first. Meryet and her family were behind Imhotep the Overseer and in front of the minor officials, who preceded the servants and the villagers. Some servants were loaded up with the possessions that Isis would take with her into the tomb. Others carried tables and trays piled high with food and flowers, jars of wine, jugs of beer and napkins for the feast that would take place after the burial.

Suddenly the courtyard stilled. The Pharaoh had arrived. With him were his daughter-queens, Meryet-Amun, Bint-Anath and Nebet-Tawy. Everyone fell to their knees and kissed the ground in respect. Meryet, who had never seen the divine Ramses before, peeked up under her eyelashes for a glimpse of the god-king. The Pharaoh was quite an old man, she realised, much older than her father, but he seemed strong and fit. His face was hawkish, with a long nose and hooded eyes. He wore a tall headdress, an intricate gold-beaded collar and a gold girdle around his tunic. His queens also wore imposing headdresses and were bedecked with priceless jewellery. They made the harem queens look like ladies-in-waiting by comparison.

Once the royal family was in place behind the bier, the procession set off for the cemetery. It was led by the *Sem*-priest, resplendent in a panther skin, followed by the Lector priest, who recited spells and prayers from a papyrus, and then a large contingent of lesser priests. The priests droned their chants and swung their censers, filling the air with the scent of frankincense. The oxen plodded behind, dragging the sled that carried the coffin. The wails and screams of the professional mourners rent the air as they tore their blue robes and hair, raked their cheeks with their nails, and threw earth on themselves to show how much the Princess would be missed.

Some of the mourners dragged the sinister *tekenu* on his sled, and the *muu* dancers capered around clapping their hands above their heads. With these strange sights and sounds, the heat and the overpowering scent of incense and flowers, the day took on an air of unreality for Meryet.

When they arrived at Isis's tomb, the mummy was removed from the coffin and propped up on a pile of sand while the *Sem*-priest performed the opening of the mouth ceremony. This ritual would restore all the Princess's bodily functions so she could enjoy the Afterlife to the full. The priest touched the face of a statue of Isis with various implements, one of them a rod with a snake's head. While chanting incantations, he made offerings of natron, incense, eye-paint, linen, food and drink, as well as the foreleg and heart of a bull.

Once these rites were completed, the mummy was placed in its nest of coffins, and the Canopic chest containing the Princess's vital organs was placed in its niche in the tomb. The servants stacked the grave goods and the protective *shabtis* around the coffin, and the priest placed a copy of the Book of the Dead on it. Only then was the tomb sealed. It was all over.

On the way home, Meryet tried to come to terms with all that had happened since Isis had fallen ill. She felt as if she had lived a whole lifetime in three months. Her mother was right: Isis's death and its aftermath had changed her. She had seen how jealousy and resentment could fester and turn into violence, and how the innocent could suffer. It had all made life seem more precarious, but also more precious.

When her parents left, Meryet returned to her workroom, tired but restless. She expected to find Miu curled up in the corner as usual, but she was not there. Meryet looked in the kitchen, but Hebeny seemed to have no idea that Meryet had even had a cat. Meryet, growing puzzled, searched the harem. But when she asked after the golden cat, people looked at her as if she'd had too much sun, insisting they'd never seen such a cat. Baffled, Meryet searched her workroom one last time, but there was not a trace of Miu, not even one golden hair.

☥

In later years, when Sethi was an important official and she was running her own cosmetics business from her home with Panehesy's help and raising her daughter, Isis, Meryet-Neith would sometimes think back on her eventful fourteenth year. When she did, she would always remember Miu and how she had appeared suddenly after the Princess's death and saved Meryet's life, only to disappear again on the very day that Isis had entered the Afterlife. She decided finally that it was one of those mysteries she would never solve, but each time she saw a golden cat, she would gaze searchingly into its eyes, hoping it was Miu.

AUTHOR'S NOTE

Meryet-Neith lived in Ancient Egypt in the nineteenth Dynasty under the reign of Ramses II, who ruled from 1304 to 1237 BC. Ramses was a great Pharaoh, who vanquished the Hittites at the Battle of Kadesh after a long and bloody war. To help cement the peace, he did take a Hittite princess as a bride in the thirty-fourth year of his reign, when he would have been in his fifties.

The Hittite princess was accorded the status of Great Royal Wife and given the Egyptian name Maathenferure. She apparently gave birth to a child and died young. There is no record of what happened to that child, whom I have reincarnated as Princess Isis. After Maathenferure died, Ramses apparently married one of her sisters. For more about the Hittites, see Trevor Bryce's *Life and Society in the Hittite World* (Oxford: Oxford University Press, 2002).

Mer-Wer, the royal harem, actually existed in the Faiyum in the Nile Delta in Lower Egypt. At various times it housed the Pharaoh's principal wives and their children, his secondary wives (who were often princesses or high-born ladies, and whose children could inherit the throne), his concubines (women of lower birth whose children could only inherit in extreme cases), foreign wives and retired royal servants. Ramses did not spend much time at *Mer-Wer*, as the royal family moved from palace to palace, each of which had its own harem. He seems to have sired about a hundred children.

Meryet's father-in-law, Ahmose, who was a doctor-priest attached to a temple, was one kind of physician practising in Ancient Egypt; the other, what we would call a general practitioner today, had no priestly duties. There were also doctors who specialised in particular branches of medicine. Ancient Egyptians suffered from diseases such as mosquito-borne malaria and schistosomiasis, a parasitic infection; epidemics of cholera and gastroenteritis; trachoma, which caused blindness; typhoid; smallpox; measles; and tuberculosis. Because they had no sugar, Egyptians' teeth were good, but were eventually ground down by the unrefined flour in their bread. For more detailed information about the practice of medicine in Ancient Egypt, see J. Worth Estes, *The Medical Skills of Ancient Egypt* (USA: Science History Publications, 1989).

If you want to know more about the mummification process and funeral rites, try Carol Andrews's *Egyptian Mummies* (London: British Museum Press, 1998). I have stuck to actual practice as closely as possible, but have exaggerated a little about the help Ahmose received from Kenamun, the Chief Embalmer, in diagnosing death by poisoning. Autopsies were not carried out in Ancient Egypt—hence some of their eccentric ideas about anatomy—but it is hard to believe that embalmers would not have learned something about the course of various diseases from the mummification process.

I must also confess to inventing the poison that killed Isis and Kyky and threatened Maya and Meryet. The major poisons in Ancient Egypt were snake and scorpion venom and the herb henbane, but there is no evidence that poison was used as a murder weapon. Most murders were the result of physical assault. I have taken the liberty of siting the murder plot in the harem because there is evidence that harems were hotbeds of intrigue. A conspiracy against Pepi I and the assassinations of at least two Pharaohs—Amenemhat I and Ramses III—were plotted in harems.

The recipes for the perfumes, oils, unguents and soaps that Meryet-Neith made come from Lise Manniche's wonderful book *Sacred Luxuries: Fragrance, Aromatherapy and Cosmetics in Ancient Egypt* (Ithaca NY: Cornell University Press, 1999). Joyce Tyldesley's *Daughters of Isis: Women of Ancient Egypt* (London: Viking, 1994) is also informative about hygiene, dress, beauty routines and jewellery as well as the position women occupied in society.

Meryet-Neith's desire to work after marriage was unusual but not unknown. High-born ladies (such as Lady Tamit) could take administrative jobs in Ancient Egypt. Some found an outlet for their creative energies in artistic home-making, gardening and charity work; others were priestesses in temples. Talented women could be dancers, musicians or acrobats. Peasant women worked at home raising their children, growing vegetables and tending animals. They prepared meals, sold goods at the markets and wove their own fabrics, making them into clothing and washing them in the river.

Life was short and often hard, as Egypt experienced cycles of good and bad seasons, but Egyptian women enjoyed unusual freedoms compared to other women in the Ancient World. They were equal to

men in the eyes of the law. This meant they could inherit, buy and sell property, make legal contracts, borrow or lend goods and initiate court proceedings, but it also meant they could be publicly tried for their crimes. The average age for Egyptian females to marry was twelve or thirteen, and males fifteen to twenty. There was no wedding ceremony as we know it; rather, the couple simply moved in together. Meryet could have expected to live until about forty, and to have two or three children.

In the nineteenth Dynasty, cats had not yet become gods. They were either pets or workers who kept down the vermin in the houses and storerooms. But, even then, they might have been ghosts …